T08246
F/FOR

This book is to be returned on or before
the last date stamped below.

21 SEP 2005

22 FEB 20

21 NOV 2005

Sept

KT-433-581

Also by Catherine Forde

Fat Boy Swim
Think Me Back
The Finding

WOODMILL HIGH SCHOOL

CATHERINE FORDE

EGMONT

T082446

F/FOR

EGMONT

We bring stories to life

First published in Great Britain 2004
by Egmont Books Ltd
239 Kensington High Street
London W8 6SA

ISBN 1 4052 0947 X

3 5 7 9 10 8 6 4

A CIP catalogue record for this title is available from the British Library

Typeset by Avon DataSet Ltd, Bidford on Avon B50 4JH
Printed and bound in Great Britain by the CPI Group

This story is dedicated to Peter McCallum (1922–2001).
My dad. My inspiration.

WOODMILL HIGH SCHOOL

AUTHOR'S NOTE

Although Grampa Dan's story is fiction, every word of his experience is based on the reality endured by Allied prisoners of war from 1942 to 1945 during the Pacific campaign of World War II.

Many Internet sites bear testimony to the horror and inhumanity endured by these soldiers, and I pray my novel does not insult their memory.

Invaluable in my research were the following books:

Second World War by Martin Gilbert (Phoenix Press, 1989).

The War Diaries of Weary Dunlop, Java and the Burma–Thailand Railway 1942–1945 by E. E. Dunlop (Nelson Publishers, 1986).

The Railway Man by Eric Lomax (Vintage, 1996).

I am most grateful to Gordon Smith, whose powers set me thinking. He gave me the link I needed between the present and the past.

CONTENTS

1	NUMBER ONE	1
2	GRAMPA'S SEND-OFF	3
3	BEST FRIENDS	16
4	THE ROVIN' EYES – PLUGGED	25
5	GRAMPA DAN CALLING	32
6	*FREE*-DOM!	41
7	HOME ALONE	55
8	SOUL FOOD	69
9	MUMMY'S HOME	74
10	ALI PATEL	80
11	WITH FRIENDS LIKE THESE . . .	89
12	AN EVENING IN THE PARK WITH GRAMPA	96
13	JUST LIKE OLD TIMES	100
14	DIGGING A HOLE	111
15	LIFE-DRAWING	121
16	RECORD BREAKERS	127
17	ROCK BOTTOM	138
18	A HAIRCUT WITH GRAMPA DAN	150
19	OPERATION ALI P	164

20	WHY DON'T YOU DO RIGHT?	176
21	HOME TRUTHS	187
22	SINGING TO MY OLD BOY'S TUNE	200
23	JUST VISITING	211
24	VIBES	215
25	JUST LIKE OLD TIMES – REVISITED	221
26	JAKEY'S PIX'N'MIX PARTY	229
27	SQUIRM, SQUIRM	240
28	CLEANING OUT MY CLOSET	252
29	BOOTING UP	266
30	THE DANGEROUS BROTHERS	274
31	THE TAPE	281
32	SECRETS AND LIES	293
33	EPIPHANY	304
34	BITING THE BULLET	310

GRAMPA DAN'S LEGACY		321
35	FALSE MEMORY SYNDROME	323
36	THE BEGINNING OF THE BEGINNING	331

1
NUMBER ONE

'Number one,' I tell the barber. 'All over.'

I'm smirking at myself in the mirror while this barber – Mister Derek, unless he's wearing the wrong poncy monogrammed jacket – drapes a nylon cape over my gear and velcroes the neck fastening. *Bit tight, ya numpty,* I nearly say, but I let it go, too busy savouring the thought of my Old Dear's soor face when I show at Grampa Dan's funeral with a skinhead.

'All over?'

Mister Derek's lips purse. I hear Jakey's voice in my head.

He'll be a poofter, same as all hairdressers. Swears he can spot one of them a mile off: *Antennae, Danny-Boy.*

'All over,' I growl, macho.

Mister Derek's got the cheek to sigh over the top of my head, shaking his own blowdried mullet. If this is the stroppy way he does business it's a wonder there's so

1

many punters queuing up on a Saturday morning to be sheared.

Both Mister Derek's hands are on my shoulders now. Paw-heavy, for a roly-poly mincer. I feel them hot through this sad black jacket my Old Boy made me wear today. I want to shrug the barber off. But I can't. His grip immobilises me in the chair.

Mister Derek's eyes hold mine in the mirror. They're blue, his pupils pinprick dots. I've seen Jakey's like that when he's on something, though never as sharp-looking as this bloke's.

His fingers grip my shoulders. 'Number one,' he sighs again. Gets the razor rasping. Doesn't say another word till he's finished.

Then he plays the usual barber joke with the soft brush, sweeping cut hair down my collar instead of on to the floor. All of a sudden he stops and leans over me, lips that close to my ear that for one hideous second I think I'm due a snog. Instead he whispers:

'Grampa Dan says, don't get your hair cut like that again, Danny. Makes you look like a prisoner of war.'

2
GRAMPA'S SEND-OFF

'You're a ned with that haircut.'

Result!

It cracks me up knowing my Old Dear is fizzing with me, but has to play things genteel, ladling out her disapproval in semaphore and hisses because we're in church.

'Danny! You're late. *Sssss*straighten that tie!'

My Old Dear's jabby index finger stilettos my arm while she fires daggers with her eyes. It's some feat: blowing an invisible gasket while you're smiling piously for the sake of mourners you hardly know. Up folk troop, tapping the Old Dear on the shoulder, whispering sympathetic claptrap in her lug.

'*Aw*ffy sorry, Susan. Poor old sowl. Must be a relief, mind.'

My Old Dear barely turns her head to see who's talking to her. Accepts condolences like she's the bloody

3

Queen, passing sympathy cards to me, as though I'm her lady-in-waiting. She keeps her eyes towards the altar. The grieving daughter-in-law. Bloody hypocrite.

'This your wee Danny, Susan? Gettin' a big lad, aren't you, son?'

Bog off!

Like my Old Dear, I fix my eyes on the altar too, trying not to see the coffin in front of it. I'm not big on small talk at the best of times.

'Your lad'll be upset, right enough, Susan, losing Grampa.'

Too right I'm upset.

Saturday morning. Ten o'clock, and I'm trussed like a black pudding in a tie and my Old Boy's jacket. New-mown hair jagging my neck. In church, for God's sake.

Again.

Should be in my pit.

Was wasted last night.

Jakey couldn't believe I'd to show up at the pineapple two days in a row.

'What for? Can't you just bury your old stiff the same night you bring him into church?'

Funerals should be at night anyway, Jakey decided. 'Up

the cemmy in the dark. Be a pure buzz, that. Anyway, Danny-Boy, now you're here, what d'you snaffle?'

We were in the park when we had this conversation last night. I showed late; didn't think I'd get out at all. Old Dear wanted me home after Grampa's box was carted into church.

'I'll need your help, Danny. Don't be disappearing off with your pals tonight.'

She'd asked all these people back to the house. Folk I'd never seen in my puff. Zimmer brigade. Sitting room was all poshed-up with trays of fancy sandwiches, and bowls of nuts that none of the gerries could chew.

Course, it wasn't the food I was after.

It was the spread on the sideboard that interested me. Groaning with bevvy, it was. Wine, beer, spirits; you name it. Probably more bevvy than Grampa Dan ever got to see in his life.

Not that he could drink: belly couldn't take booze.

'Guts are knackered, Danny. Bloody Japs.'

When I saw the swally my folks had bought in for his send-off, I was glad I hadn't shot straight from the church to the park after all. *Cheers, Grampa Dan*.

*   *   *

'Sherry? That the best you could do, man?'

'It's a full bottle, Jakey.'

I'd been lucky to slope out with the sherry at all, but there was no point in trying to explain that to Jakey. Old Dear had left it in the kitchen by mistake. Rest of the booze was under the lock and key of her nippy wee eyes.

I could have sworn my Old Boy clocked me sneaking out with the bottle tucked up my jook while he sneaked a sly fag with his sad teacher mates in the garden. I nearly said to him, *If you were that desperate for a smoke you should have tapped me.*

He didn't call me back – knows it's a waste of time asking where I think I'm off to at this hour, son. Wouldn't want me to give him a showing-up in front of his pals.

Mind you, the way I'm feeling at the funeral, I might yet be giving him a showing-up. Jakey mixed my sherry with some past-its-sell-by-date cider that Waz's mum had chucked out. Couple of times in church I almost have to make a lavvy dash; technicolor-yawn job threatening.

Still, a hangover takes my mind off the *drone drone drone* of Grampa Dan's big send-off.

A—bide with me . . .

I mean, Jesus! Whose idea was that? Grampa Dan hated all that pious stuff. Hymns. Prayers. Never went near a church. If he couldn't get his fingers to work the buttons quickly enough when *Songs of Praise* came on, he'd fling the remote at the telly.

'Bollocks!'

I'd hear him through the wall when I was triple-checking my art homework was tip-top for Miss West at the last-Sunday-night-minute and I'd have to get myself in quickstyle to sort him out.

'Turn that cack off, Danny. Yon Aled-ulias holier-than-thous don't know what they're talking about. Give us Ella Fitzgerald instead.'

Too right, Grampa.

Why isn't her voice filling the church mellow today instead of dry old hymns he hated?

Every time we say goodbye, I die a little.

Ella, Peggy, Billie, Hoagy, Louis, Duke, Frank . . .

I know the soundtrack to Grampa Dan's life. Could have made a farewell tape, no bother.

Since I'm thinking music, still struggling at keeping

down the boke, I test myself on the lyrics of Skarr's latest CD:

> *Shaved and broken*
> *Crack the whip,*
> *See them fall,*
> *Kommandant, Kempetai.*
> *Ribs and bones*
> *Ribs and bones.*

I superimpose Seth Lamprey's vocals over some old geezer, top heavy with a stack of medals, who's whingeing on the pulpit about '*A time for dying, A time for living . . .*'

How about a time for putting a sock in it, matey? I suggest, telepathically. But alas, Grampa's last gig's barely rolling.

No sooner has Medal Man shuffled back to his pew than my Old Boy's bounding to the mike. He's all dickied up in a new black suit, last three hairs on his pate slicked back with *my* wax. He's got ten o'clock shadow: the too-grief-stricken-to-shave designer-stubble look.

At least he spares us his happy-clappy guitar. He's only reading in church today, giving *The Lord's My Shepherd* big licks in his by-the-way-I'm-a-teacher voice. Except he

8

can't hack it. I'm busy cranking up Seth's voice –

> *Break them*
> *Break them*
> *Take their soul*
> *Make them*
> *Make them*
> *YOU control –*

– when my Old Boy loses it. His voice cracks. Great snottery sobs surge all the way up from his last-chance-trendy Chelsea boots and pour out, blubbering, into the mike.

'*In the Lord's own house sh-sh-shall I dwell* . . . I'm sorry,' he falters, in a sort of bleaty voice, very apt, given the context of his reading. Geddit: shepherd, sheep? And he's looking at me.

What's he want me to do? Go up there and rescue him? *There, there, Daddykins.*

No chance, Padre. Anyway, the Old Dear's fussing plenty for the both of us, producing paper hankies to dab his runny nose like he's three years old. Kidding on she gives a damn.

Things quieten down after that. The priest, who clearly never clapped eyes on my Grampa Dan in his puff, struggles to dredge up something appropriate to say. The words *clutching* and *straws* spring to my mind as we're served a plate of tripe about Grampa Dan.

'Here was a man who endured unspeakable torture in the service of his country, but who wasn't broken. His faith sustained him in his darkest hours. Daniel Hennessy was a true soldier of Christ.

'And . . .

'Er . . .'

That's all folks.

'Bollocks.'

Yup. That's what Grampa Dan would have said.

Or maybe he'd have said, 'I did what I had to do to stay alive, nothing more.'

My Old Boy wrote that in the tribute he isn't fit to make now, quoting Grampa Dan.

I did what I had to do to stay alive, nothing more.

That struck me, because Grampa Dan never, *ever* said anything to me about what happened to him in the war. And I always thought I'd get round to asking him about it one day. Like a lot of things I think I'll get round to . . .

'Danny!'

The jaggiest bit of my Old Dear's elbow interrupts my guest drum solo with Skarrs at Madison Square Garden. Everyone's up on their feet, except me – and Grampa Dan. The priest's having a whale of a time to himself, swinging the old incense, and splashing us all awake with Holy Water.

'*Eternal rest, grant unto him, O Lord . . .*' he drones.

Then.

Alleluia!!!!! It's all over.

We're walking out, Old Dear and I first behind the coffin. It's shoogling about something awful, none of the pall-bearers the same height. Two undertakers are at the front. One's taller than my Old Boy, but the other bloke – the boss man, who probably always gets in front – he's a midget. Old Boy's at the back, with Medal Man. They're clutching on to each other's shoulders, trying to keep Grampa's back end straight. Poor old Medal Man's puffing under the strain, probably thinking to himself, won't be long till I'm the one getting the bumpy ride in the big pencil case. I can see the bones of his knuckles

11

poking white through his skin as he claws the shoulder of my Old Boy's new jacket. He's puffing as though he's lifting weights instead of a wee wafer light as Grampa Dan was at the end.

It's cheek forcing an old geezer like Medal Man to carry a coffin.

What was wrong with me?

I'm tall as my Old Boy now, easy.

All they had to do was ask.

We're edging down the aisle now and the congregation's singing: *Jesus remember me when I come into Your kingdom*, over and over and over like no one can be bothered going on to a second verse.

Folk at the back are out of synch with the ones up the front. Bit Goth, the effect, specially since my own head is suddenly swirling fit to burst with the intro to another tune altogether: Grampa's number one song of all time. Hoagy Carmichael's 'Stardust'.

'Listen to that melody, Danny. Isn't it something?' I can even hear Grampa say, same as he did every time 'Stardust' played, and I wish – just one more time – we could all hear what he never tired of hearing. Just the way he heard it.

At the echo of his voice I have to stare right hard at my Old Boy. He's walking in front of me, making an effort to join in the final hymn, but giving up after a few notes. The shoulder not carrying the coffin's going up and down like it does when he's laughing hysterically about something only he finds funny.

My Old Dear rubs one hand across the Old Boy's back (her loving-wife routine don't fool me), then – major grossout – gropes out her other hand for mine. She's crying. Can't think why. After the things she said about Grampa Dan.

I yank my arm away.

At the back of the church stand another couple of old geezers, same vintage as Medal Man. They don't reach out to touch the coffin as it passes, or bless themselves like most of the other rosary-clacking folk I've clocked. They salute.

And so does Richard – Dicky-Head, as Jakey says we've to call him.

Haven't seen him for months.

And I pretend not to see him now, staring hard at the brass crucifix on top of Grampa's coffin until it swims before my eyes.

Richard, wee Richard. Havenae seen you for yon time. Not so wee any more, either, all grown up in your uniform. Only seems like yesterday you were in here every day. You and Danny all over my bed like measles.

Now you want me to talk into your machine. It's not on the now, is it? Because I canny think what you want me to say. That's a laugh, eh? I'm laid here good enough for nothing more than thinking, and I'm looking at the telly, or my tranny's on and I hear a word – *Japanese. Prisoner. Work camp* – and I canny help myself. All these memories flood back. Things I don't remember remembering. Things I don't want to remember. They play in my head and they won't switch off.

Not that I think there's any point you talking to me if you want proper history. I never did anything brave or important.

Survived.

That's it.

I mean, these wee scars you and Danny kept

pestering me about werenae from battle. Any combat I've seen's been on telly. David Niven, John Wayne, Kenneth More doing soldiers better than anyone I ever met for real... There was no fighting in my war. These scars on my hands are for drawing pictures.

I was just a driver. Dan the Van in civvy street. Corporal Hennessy, truck driver in the army. What else could I do? Nineteen when I went in, twenty when I was captured, older than I feel these days when I got out. You should have seen me, Richard. I didnae know myself. Same as I don't know Danny the now.

3
BEST FRIENDS

My Old Boy's having another fag. Out in the open this time, checking the undertakers slide Grampa Dan into the hearse properly. Old Boy's shoulders are pulled up to his ears and he stamps from foot to foot as though he's cold despite the sun. His smoking hand shakes.

My Old Dear's not crying any more. She's sobbing. Making a right show of herself. There's a cluster of her pals round her, tarted up as if they're at a desperado's hen night instead of a funeral. Shades. Red lips. High heels. Token black tights . . .

They're all talking at once while their eyes rove the church, checking to see if there's any talent hidden among the OAPs.

The saluters make their way on to the pavement, all hobbling, taking the stairs carefully, using the handrail. These old blokes wear medals too, though none are in the same league as Medal Man. Hopeless Hope I hear him introduce himself, shaking hands with Richard.

I watch all this, well out of sight behind a pillar, enjoying my own nicotine rush, first of the day. First of many, now the Old Boy's in the tar club again. My Old Dear'll think any ciggie smell's coming from him.

My Old Boy's shaking hands with Medal Man and the other saluters before they toddle to their cars. Richard steps back from the conversation, listening, but not intruding. Looks about twenty-five in his blazer. A man, despite the schoolbag over his shoulder. Not a dweeby third year, same age as myself.

I can see my Old Dear's got her Dan-scan going, sweeping the thinning crowd of mourners for her wayward spawn. Lips that angry, tight way they go when she's on my case. Course, I stay put. It's a beast watching her get her knickers in a twist.

The Old Boy sifts the mourners now. 'Seen my son? Skinhead?'

Before I can saunter out, all devil-may-care, Richard points to me. I see him mouthing, 'Behind that pillar,' as my Old Boy claps him on the shoulder.

'Thanks for coming, Richard. Appreciated.'

Anyone else who shopped me like that would be

a grass, but that's just Richard being Richard.

Best friends.

That's what we were.

'Joined at the bloomin' hip, you two,' Grampa Dan would josh when we jammed each other at the bedroom door, fighting to get in and see him first.

Mates since playgroup. Age three, just out of nappies. Meeting at the colouring-in table. We stayed together, through nursery, then primary. Inseparable. Living in the same cul-de-sac, near enough to walk in and out of each other's houses as if they were extensions of our own.

Danny and Richard.

Richard and Danny.

Thought we'd be best friends forever. Death do us part. We didn't bore each other. We didn't compete with each other. We just got on great.

Until secondary school. My parents separated us and everything changed.

Your folks always think they know what's best but they're clueless.

That's what Jakey says. Not about the Richard

thing, because he doesn't know about that, but about parents in general. He's right, of course. If Richard had sat the entrance exam and come to the Academy with me, I wouldn't be in so much bother all the time. I wouldn't be bored. I wouldn't be in all the dumbo sets. I *definitely* wouldn't be one of Jakey's crowd, because he hates Richard.

Laugh is, before I started my posh school, Richard was the one who promised things wouldn't change. 'Why should they? We'll get together when we get home, same as usual. There's every weekend. And the holidays.'

When I first started at the Academy, it seemed Richard was right enough about nothing changing. Neither of us mentioned our schools when we met up. Then, a few weeks into term I'd go round for Richard and be sent away with a flea in my ear. His Old Dear policing the door.

'Richard's doing his homework, Danny. Haven't you got piles to do yourself?'

Then I'd get: 'Don't want Richard out during the week. Leave it till Friday. He'll phone.'

We never phoned each other.

His voice would sound alien down the line. He'd say,

'I'll probably see you at the weekend, Danny.'

But come Saturday morning: 'Sorry, Danny. Richard's playing rugby.'

'Afternoon, then?'

'He's got a sleepover, Danny. Someone's birthday. All the boys are going. You must be meeting lots of other boys and girls, too.'

'Yeah,' I'd say.

Truth is, except for Miss West, my art teacher, no one went out of their way to get to know me at the Academy. Don't know why I didn't make new friends. Never needed to before. Didn't have the knack, maybe.

Or maybe I blew it. In the first week, a couple of the lads told me to bring my trainers in and play footie at lunchtime. I turned up – minus trainers – had a game, but wasn't invited a second time. Course I was being trialled. Should have made more of an effort. All the footie guys were mates out of school; decent enough with it. They went to the game on Saturdays, booked five-a-side courts on Sundays . . .

Jakey Wilson was the only other boy who didn't play football.

We probably wouldn't have got together otherwise.

Would still be Danny and Richard.

Richard and Danny. WOODMILL HIGH SCHOOL

'Really *nice* of Richard to come to the funeral. Grampa was *very* fond of him,' growls my Old Dear. We're trailing Grampa's hearse on his last journey, chauffeur-driven in a sleek limousine. Since her words snarl round me like an accusation, and my Old Boy has insisted on sitting up front with the driver and the privacy window shut, I take it the Old Dear must think she's talking to me. So I twist myself as far away from her voice as I can get without undoing my seat belt and dislocating my neck from my shoulders.

'They saw a fair bit of each other in the last few weeks,' I tell myself I can't hear her say.

But that's news to me! If I could have asked *when* and *why* Richard had seen Grampa without actually talking to my Old Dear, I might have done it. But I was already stinging enough from one of her unprovoked verbal parries.

Nice.

21

Dangerous word, that, when my Old Dear uses it around me. Sharp as a nunchaka it is.

I block anything else she says – something about Richard's history project – watching our funeral limo snake the maze of pathways in the cemetery. How does the driver know where to go? All these gravestones look the same. How will we tell Grampa Dan from anyone else? How will we ever find him again?

'Fine-looking big boy, Richard.'

Not like some folk I could mention. Don't need to be in MENSA to get the Old Dear's inference. I don't even need to look at her. I can tell her mouth's twisted in disappointment by the way she's talking.

You separated us, you stupid cow. That was nice, too.

'You'll miss him, Danny,' Grampa Dan said when he heard we were going to different schools. 'Good friends are priceless.'

You'll have to let me off on dates, Richard. Canny even mind my army number, but I'm grand with names when it comes to folk. Their faces are still in my head all these years on. I'll say yon's Mack or Sammy Orr or Hopeless. We're talking what? Sixty-five years, and counting. All those faces. And other faces whose names I never knew. They're still here. In my noddle.

Smiling. Joking. Scared. Skinny. Bloated. Sick. Dead.

I'm talking to you the now and I've got Big Taff Murray in my head. Leaning on his shovel, squinting up at me. He's wiping sweat off his face. Half dead from digging. Checking under his oxter – like we all did – case Fat Guard catches him slacking. Lands him one with his fancy swagger stick...

'DIG!'

Taff's like a matchstick man, handle of his shovel thicker than his arm. You'd wonder he could still stand up. A bloody sin. And I tell you, he didnae look like that when we were first billeted together, Richard. Him a big rugby player from the Welsh valleys, and I'm not talking your posh school rugger type. Taff was a miner, prop for his village team. I tell you there's something no' right about a lunk like Taff shrivelling to a skeleton in a loincloth before your eyes.

And him a rock to me from day one of our capture.

'We'll get to see an International yet, Henny, boyo,' Taff promised me when the Japs marched us out of Rangoon.

4
THE ROVIN' EYES – PLUGGED

Although, without his body, Grampa Dan's shindig isn't a proper wake, it's keeping me a-wake all right.

It's hours since all these liggers crammed every downstairs room to scoff my Old Dear's steak pie and swill free bevvy.

What a nightmare of a day. Home planet invaded by yammering life forms, all dressed in black. Since I don't have a chromosome in common with these aliens, I repel any advances with my usual strategy. It's hysterical how people bodyswerve you if you grunt and twitch a bit, like you're a *special* boy, as my Old Boy calls the kids in adult bodies he teaches art to. Not that I'm off the hook. Old Dear has me running round like a blue-arsed fly. Taking coats, recycling those nuts the gerries spat out last night, and keeping drinks topped up. Every time I make a bid for the sanctuary of my room – earphones on, sketchbook out, leave the world behind – the Old Dear nabs me. 'Where d'you think you're going, Danny?'

Must be all the swally swilling around, but no one's in any hurry to leave, apart from the rellies on my Old Dear's side who split after a couple of dry sherries and an hour of muttering darkly about the Hennessys. Soon as they're offski it's like someone sticks that Pink song on: 'Get the Party Started'. Out with the good whisky, off with the ties.

Funerals, eh? Dead funny.

I mean, I never knew my Old Boy could let his hair down. Well, literally he can't, since he's balder than Homer Simpson, but no sooner has he seen his in-laws out than he's hi-fiving (cringe) two suits who, when I'd been passing round the cheesy puffs, gave me this middle-aged *What d'you wanna be when you leave school, Danny? Your dad tells us you're a bit of an artist* crap. Suddenly these same suits are setting up a sax and a bass while my Old Boy plugs in the amp he told me was too powerful for our circuit board. When he tunes up his Les Paul, he keeps a fag just hanging and no more out the side of his mouth, *so* Keith Richards you'd swear he hadn't married the anti-smoking dragon. Not only that, he pulls his shirt out, unbuttons it, forgetting his waistband's pushing fifty.

Then he strikes a chord. Not a Kumbaya, school folk-Mass chord. But a broken glass, leather-jacket-and-Jack-Daniels gargle of a chord.

The Rovin' Eyes were playing suburbia.

I always knew my Old Boy could play guitar. If my Old Dear was off the scene and Grampa Dan was asleep, he'd get his guitar out and tune up one of his old ones for me. He'd try to teach me chords, riffs, twelve-bar blues, his fingers flying over the strings. He'd make it look easy, but it's not. Not for me. I was – I am – hopeless: clumsy, rotten at strumming, worse at picking, with no ear for what the next chord should be. I must have stormed out of every lesson.

Not once did the Old Boy come after me, calling me back to try again. He hates confrontation. Would rather stay put, hunched over his guitar, playing quiet as a secret, than flex his paternal muscles.

Meek and spineless, the Old Dear's called him in the past. That's why I can't figure out what's come over him tonight. He'd stop playing the nanosecond Grampa Dan banged the floor for something. Even sooner if the Old Dear's key scraped the lock, jumping up so fast that I could hear all his strings yowl in panic as he dumped the guitar back on its stand, kidding on he hadn't been anywhere near it.

So, I knew he could play, but not like this. Headbanging, greasy rock'n'roll. Three old men singing 'Sweet Little Sixteen'. None of it's my cup of tea, you understand, but not bad for a group of dinosaurs fifteen years off their pension.

Old Dear was beelin' when the music started.

'What d'you think you're doing?' she hisses at my Old Boy in that flesh-corroding tone she usually saves for me.

'What's it look like?' Old Boy replies, cranking up his amp to eleven at least. 'Gonna play.'

'Shouldn't you be showing a bit more respect for your dad, Paul? This is a solemn occasion.'

'Away you go. I gave him a lifetime of respect.'

Hours later, the Rovin' Eyes are still giving it laldy, doing requests for all the red-wine-drinking art teachers who turned up at the funeral from my Old Boy's Adult

Education college and never went back to work.

In the kitchen, with the door shut against the Rovin' Eyes, my Old Dear's in vodka therapy. When I stick my head in to say I'm hitting the sack, I interrupt one of her Just Divorced pals in the middle of a drunken lecture: 'Y'don't need this crap any more, Susan. He'sh dead and you were here for him. Juzz go if you're unhappy. Y'owe Paul nothin' and wee Danny'sh a big boy now.'

You could cut the silence with a switchblade when I appeared. Five suicide blondes swivelling their heads round to glower at me while the Rovin' Eyes played 'Leaving on a Jet Plane'.

'G'night,' I say, but nobody answers.

Japs marched us out of Rangoon after the army surrendered. That was the start, but get this straight now, Richard: there was nothing glorious about my war. Or noble. If you want a hero you've got the wrong fella. Whole business was a rug pulling me arse over tip. No sooner do I get my land legs back after sailing halfway round the world from Scotland to Calcutta, than it's taking me all my bottle to acclimatise to the heat, insects, and bloody rice rice rice. Next thing we're upping sticks. *You're going to Rangoon, boys. Japs getting too big for their boots. Need more Brits in Burma to show the Nip who's boss.*

When you're no more than a wee Jo Soldier that's how the COs tell you you're mobilising. No other info. *Japs getting too big for their boots.* Bloody understatement of the war. They were overrunning the Pacific like rats. By the time we're off the truck in Rangoon we're told we've surrendered. Decision made way up the ranks like every other decision that affected me in the bloody war. When you're no more than cannon fodder, Richard, no one tells you a dicky bird.

Get behind the white flag, you're ordered.

March.

You're POWs now, and your war's over.

See what I'm saying about having the wrong fella if you want a hero? All I did was surrender. No wonder the Japs treated us the way they did. They were disgusted their enemy could give up arms without a fight. They'd rather take themselves out with a grenade, or bayonet their own bellies, than sit out a war as some other country's trophy.

5
GRAMPA DAN CALLING

Bang Bang Bang.

I'm imagining. Half asleep. Must be imagining Grampa Dan's stick banging his floor while Mr Patel from over the road does a better job of murdering 'Delilah' than Tom Jones ever did. There must be a wee chip in my head associating noise in the house with the rhythm of Grampa Dan's protest.

He had two rhythms.

One: Bang Bang Bang was for racket, which he hated. The other was a relentless BANGBANGBANG BANGBANGBANG that did your head in. He'd keep that going until someone went up to sort him. Japanese water torture, my Old Boy called it.

When Grampa banged like that, it could be anything he wanted. Something important: 'Commode. Quick, son.' Or trivial: 'Is that clock straight on the shelf, Danny?'

I used to guess what he was after before I went in.

'Dropped my specs.'

'Any new drawings for my wall?'

'Who was that on the phone?'

'Give us your chat, Danny.'

When I imagine the stick banging tonight, I jump automatically.

I've not been in Grampa's room since I found him, a week ago. The door's been shut. I haven't felt like opening it.

He didn't snuff it in there, though I thought he had. He was that white, that cold, I didn't even bother feeling for a pulse. Nearly pulled his cover up over his face because his eyes were open and I didn't like them staring at me. Course they were staring at me because he was alive and couldn't bang with his stick any more. That's why I'd gone into his room in the first place. There hadn't been a cheep from him for hours. I was next door, sketching out a still life for art homework (glass, toothbrush, comb) and cranking up Seth's vocals louder than I'd ever done without headphones. I was wondering how the heck I was getting away with it. Thinking Grampa Dan must have gone deaf, although there was never, ever anything wrong with his hearing.

> *On your knees you beasts of war.*
> *Paying for your country's crimes.*
> *Wallow in your filth and gore*
> *Beg for life*
> *And beg some*
> *MORE!!!*

'Keep talking to him,' the paramedic said in the ambulance. 'Hearing's the last sense to go.'

Grampa didn't even make it to the hospital. Pegged out while we weaved through the rush hour, siren screaming too loud for me to say anything worthwhile. Paramedic said he wouldn't have suffered.

They don't know the half of it, my Old Boy said.

I'm not stupid. I know fine Grampa Dan's not here any more but when I open his door it feels as if he is. Like the sound of his banging stick, my brain's so programmed to seeing him, swallowed up in his bed, whiter than his pillows, that it's harder to believe the bare mattress I'm looking at is the reality, and the picture I see of him floating in my head is the hologram, the fake.

The room still pongs of his bedsmell. It's hard to describe. Maybe everyone's is different. Grampa Dan's bedsmell is – was – a sort of digestive biscuits in the false teeth mingled with fart build-up under the covers and too much central heating. Not pleasant, but like cutting his toenails, you got used to it.

He'd have been banging all right if he could hear the racket downstairs tonight. Struggling to raise himself. *'Turn that down!'*

Too right, Grampa Dan.

Some woman who thinks she's Shirley Bassey's giving it 'Come Up and See Me, Make Me Smile', while my Old Boy's guitar tries to drown her out. There's nothing to absorb the noise up here. Old Dear's swiped the bedclothes already – probably burned them – and taken the curtains down. The racket from downstairs bounces off the walls with nothing to muffle it. Everything's distorted as though I'm trapped in an echo chamber.

Taxis are lining up outside, horns parping. One of the drivers is thumping the front door with his fist, beckoning me down when he sees me at Grampa's window. *No chance*, I mouth at him. Keeping my forehead pressed to the glass, I switch focus from the street outside to the bare room stretching behind me.

People are rolling out on to the street now, dithering over the taxis until more arrive, some dame being sick on the pavement. Sax and bass step round her without saying anything to my Old Dear. My Old Boy doesn't show at all. He's picking out some tune to himself, the wail of his guitar filling the house like it's crying.

I take it everyone's gone when my Old Dear starts to shout downstairs, and I hear glass smash. In my echo chamber, I don't know what she's saying because my Old Boy plays over her.

No. There'd be none of that shouting tonight if Grampa Dan was here. Only dirty looks and enough of an atmosphere to set up an earth annexe on Mars. Now he's dead, my folks can shout all they like. Who's to stop them?

'Not me,' I whisper into the mirror on Grampa Dan's chest of drawers. When I was wee I'd hold it for him and we'd natter while he shaved. For the last couple of years he'd have to give it the full-throttle bangbangbangbang before I'd chuck it on his bed as I headed for school.

When I tilt the mirror I can see the room behind me – the bare mattress, the bedside cabinet, the wall covered with all my best school artwork over the years. No matter how much the corners curled or the pencil drawings faded, Grampa refused to let my Old Dear take a single picture down.

'Leave them be, Susan. They're magic.'

Whatever way I turn it, the mirror seems to catch a glint of movement in the room like someone's coming up behind me. Course there's no one. Just my face filling the glass, funny looking with all my hair off.

'Makes you look like a prisoner of war.'

Mister Derek's barmy words come into my head.

A barber I'd never seen in my life before.

He knew my name.

I didn't even think twice about it at the time, my head looping from Jakey's cocktail hangover.

'Grampa Dan says, don't get your hair cut like that again, Danny.'

What was he talking about? And more to the point, why the hell am I thinking about it now, up here on my

37

own in the room where Grampa Dan as good as died?

I'm out of there. Not before I get the Old Dear to quit shouting. I pick up Grampa Dan's stick, still hanging on his bedpost: Bang Bang Bang.

Hundreds of us blokes shuffled quiet, like a big tame snake through Rangoon. I suppose we were all worried, wondering what would happen, now someone else was cracking the whip. Some could hide their anxiety better than others. Whistling through their teeth, muttering curses while the Japs herded us up and marched us off. None of that bravado with me, Richard. I was in a right state. Rough, the Japs were. Their attitude. Tone of their voices. You might not know what they were saying, but you understood loud and clear.

And we all had our own take on our captors. There was talk they were wiping out anyone in their path – bairns, women, old folk. Razing villages to the ground if there was a whiff of resistance.

There were rumours: rape, slaughter, forced labour.

Aye, that'll be right, most of us thought. Scaremongering.

Some of our lads said they'd heard the Japs gave POWs a hard time. Canny be true, we said.

'Baloney!' said Sammy Orr. I can see him spluttering the word into his tea, the very morning we were rounded up. If we were taken – and we won't be – he said, the Japs would stick to the rules. Follow international protocol. Same as if we took *them* prisoner. Otherwise there was no point in the bloody Geneva Convention, was there? And Sammy'd tell us something else for nothing: under the skin we were all pawns in a war none of us started. Same as every war before or since. Japs'd respect that.

'Different sides of the same coin we are, lads.'

Bollocks.

Those Japs were a different currency altogether, most of them.

I'll tell you what they did to Sammy Orr, will I, Richard? Him and his Geneva Convention.

6
FREE-DOM!

'There's no scran in this house.'

Jakey's not happy. He tips the scatterings from the lone cornflakes packet he's found on to the floor. There's a cracking sound from the worktop he's standing on. I nearly tell him to get down.

'Sorry,' I say instead, opening the fridge for the umpteenth time on the off chance my wishful thinking might have magicked up some bacon.

Mud from Jakey's boots slimes the worktops after he jumps on to the cornflakes packet. Bang. He kicks the crushed box into the air. It lands on the mountain of dishes in the sink, knocking a teacup to the floor. Smash!

'Any dosh then, Danny-Boy?'

'Just for the bus and school tomorrow.'

'We're doggin' it tomorrow. It's Friday. C'mon, we'll get chips.'

I trail Jakey to the chippy. We don't talk. He's on his

41

mobile telling Sean and Waz where to be later. 'Park. Bring cash. Danny-Boy's skint.'

At the chippy Jakey snaps his fingers, holding out his hand for my money. I wait outside while he goes in, still talking on his mobile.

A few days after Grampa's funeral my Old Dear split, so I've been seeing a lot of Jakey, no questions asked. He's been in the house, staying over the last few nights. Don't think my Old Boy realises yet. Old Dear would freak if she knew, not that we're likely to be chitter-chattering about my social calendar when she bothers her ginger to phone.

I didn't invite Jakey to stay. He just came back after the park with me and didn't go home. He can do that, he says. His Old Dear's in Florida mostly; new boyfriend. Big brother Nut's meant to be in charge of him.

First time Jakey stayed over, we were up all night. He'd taken something Nut's mate had sold him. Couldn't stop talking. Load of gibberish that I thought would have put the wind up my Old Boy, but he didn't even glance from his guitar when Jakey burst into the sitting room. Old Boy's eyes were shut, headphones on, cigarette dangling out of his mouth. Jakey nicked a couple of fags from under his nose, gave him the vicky.

My Old Boy doesn't notice anything these days: the empty cupboards, the dirty dishes, the Ben Nevis of laundry in front of the washing machine.

Doesn't even notice if I dog school – and him a teacher too. That's how bad things are since my Old Dear upped sticks. I reckon he's got his own preoccupations. He's been sleeping on the couch. Leaves for work before I'm out my scratcher.

'Better get up, Danny,' is the extent of his parental input.

I don't want to dog it again this week. I'd to do it on Monday – missed art – because Jakey was in some state after the pill he'd popped. He wouldn't stop puking. Tuesday, I was so knackered I didn't hear my Old Boy wake me (maybe he never bothered). Slept in till lunchtime. Jakey was sleeping too. He'd my bed. I woke when Gubby phoned the house, looking for me, and I kidded him I'd the runs. He wanted me to put the Old Dear on. I'd to say she'd left home and I didn't have a number for her.

Now Gubby wants to speak to me off the record

before he hauls in the Old Boy. If I dog it, I'll be on report and every bloody teacher'll be on my back: attendance cards, detention, counselling. Things I need like itching powder down my kecks. I'll have to go in, even though it looks like I'll be walking and going hungry.

Whatever Jakey's bought with my money at the chippy, he's scoffed. Although his cheeks are bursting, he shovels more and more food into his mouth, face clatted in tomato sauce. Still talking – or should I say spitting – into the mobile, he watches me watching him through the chip shop window.

'Filled a wee space, that. Here, Danny.' When Jakey's eaten his fill, I get the cold hard leftover chips and a scrap of batter stuck in a dollop of tomato sauce.

Smacking his belly, Jakey strides the street in front of me, lighting one of my Old Boy's fags.

Although my legs follow him, my head slows down. I should go home. I could clear up a bit, figure out the washing machine, sort through the schoolwork Gubby wants to see tomorrow. Get a bit of drawing done.

Old Dear might phone. I wish . . . Do I wish?

She hasn't been in touch since she left. Not directly.

None of her pals are saying where she is. Only that she's fine, better than fine . . .

'What you dawdlin' for?'

Jakey hangs back until I'm alongside him, then grabs my neck in an armlock and rubs my nose with his knuckles. I hate that.

'If that puggy's still broke we'll get drink money,' he says, yanking me into the amusement arcade we were barred from last weekend. 'Keep edgy.'

The arcade manager yells he's calling the cops this time. He was on to us like a shot when he heard the puggy chink open, coins spilling everywhere. Now I'm really cursing myself for not going home after the chippy. My Old Dear'll kill my Old Boy if she gets to hear about this.

'Name?' The manager asks me first, although he's holding Jakey by the arm.

'Danny Hennessy,' I say.

'Toss-pot.' Jakey scowls at me, fighting the manager's grip.

'*Your* name, son?'

'John Smith,' Jakey lies, cool as you like. *Watch and learn, Danny-Boy.*

'Address?'

45

I've never heard of the place Jakey gives. Neither has the manager. He marches him to the office, calling for someone to grab a hold of me before I scoot. That's when Jakey goes mental, thrashing and screaming. 'You're breaking my arm, mister. Gerrofff. I've done nuthin'. Hennessy burst the puggy.'

Jakey's bawling his head off, yanking free of the manager, pointing at me, making sure everyone in the arcade hears the racket.

In the confusion the manager loses his grip on Jakey. He doesn't know what to do next: catch him again, go for me instead, get on the blower to the cops . . . ?

He's yelling, 'Stay there.'

Jakey's yelling too. 'You assaulted me. I'll get you done,' and I hear my own voice in there somewhere whining, 'It wasn't me.'

Somewhere in the midle of this rammy, Jakey legs it, dragging me after him.

'Thanks a bundle for dropping me in it there, Jakey,' I gulp, breathless. We ran all the way back to my place from the arcade.

'My pleasure.' Jakey grins, stacking ten pences into

pounds. When he *does* look up he's not grinning any longer.

'Why the hell d'you give that suit your real name? Do that again to me and you're dead. Yo!'

My phone's at Jakey's elbow. Soon as it rings he answers.

'Who? Danny? Nah! Wrong number . . . Who's callin'? Oh it's *you*, Dicky-Head?'

Jakey drops the receiver on its cradle. Continues counting his money without a word. Eventually he tuts.

'Why you still seeing that Dicky-Boy Dickhead, Danny-Boy?'

What you answering my phone for? 'I don't, Jakey,' my mouth snorts.

The phone rings again.

I lunge for it. Too late.

'Told you, Dicky-Head, no Danny here. Piss off.'

But it's not Richard this time.

Jakey pulls a face, holding the phone away as if it might chew his ear. I hear sharp tones.

'Je-*sus*. Some nippy sweetie for you.'

Jakey makes sure he speaks clearly into the receiver before he hands it to me.

'Who is that, Danny?'

Old Dear sounds miles away. An echo on the line.

'Friend.'

'Where's Dad?'

'Out. Dunno.'

There's a shaky sigh. 'God –' Then, 'Are you all right?'

I can hardly make out the Old Dear's voice, she's gone so quiet.

'What?' Impatience floods me. 'Can't hear you?'

'Are you all right, Danny?' Now she's whispering, maybe even crying.

'Whass*uuuuup*, darlin'?'

Jakey butts my head aside, and shouts down the phone. When I try to jerk the receiver back, he shoves me off balance and leaves the room, slamming the door at his back. I hear him breathing down the extension in the kitchen.

'How's Dad, Danny?'

What can I say? *As if you care? Soon as Grampa Dan snuffed it you were offski. Don't even tell us where you've gone.*

'Awright.'

'Are you managing OK for food and things?'

'Mnnn.'

My mumble is drowned by a puff of indignation from Jakey on the other line.

'Look, who *is* that, Danny? I hope it's not that . . .'

'Just a mate,' I cut her off before she mentions the name on the tip of her tongue. 'Put the phone down,' I call through to Jakey, covering the receiver with my hand. 'Gonna, please?' *Please!*

No chance. I hear Jakey mouth-breathe louder than ever.

There's a long three-way silence. Valuable time ticking away.

I mean, it's not that there aren't one or two pressing matters I'd like to discuss with my Old Dear.

Where are you?

Are you coming back?

But I know there's no point. At the best of times I can't talk to her. And I wouldn't dare now with Jakey on the line, whistling the chorus of Skarr's *You Waste My Time, Bitch* through his teeth:

> *Don't tie me with your conversations*
> *Why don't you get to HELL?*

Please don't sing, Jakey, I'm praying.

'Is that boy still listening in?'

The Old Dear's voice is tight and thin now.

'Sure am, ma'am,' Jakey drawls.

'Some friend you are,' she says, in her full-on Mrs Angry voice.

Jakey mimics the Old Dear's voice, *'Some friend . . .'* but she cuts through him.

'Danny.' Clear as a bell. No more trembles. 'Tell your father I phoned and I'll be round. I love you.'

'When?'

I can't believe how loudly I yell, nearly drowning out Jakey's falsetto, 'Oooh, I love you too, Mummy. Jeez, you nearly deafened me there, Danny-Boy. What you shoutin' for? Oul bitch is gone.'

Jakey shoves me on to the settee, fist to my chest. He laughs.

'Christ, you're well shot of her.'

I'd be lying if I said I stand up for my Old Dear. Even if I wanted to, I couldn't have done. All the wind was knocked out of me, and it wasn't just from Jakey's punch.

Hearing my Old Dear's voice again, out of the blue, I can't describe the way I feel. Happy. Sad. Angry. Lonely. Screwed up, basically. I still don't think I like her.

I love you she'd said, same as she used to say every

night, no matter how much shit we'd flung at each other that day. Words must have choked her as the years went on. Wonder if she knew she was nicking a leaf out of Grampa Dan's book of wisdom. *Never let the sun go down on your anger, Danny,* he'd tell me. *Harder than you think, sometimes.*

I love you, she'd said.

Love you back, I used to reply. But that was years ago.

'You're no' listenin', dough-heid. I'm away up the park.'

Jakey's been filling his pockets with the puggy cash. Then he opens our sideboard drawer, looking for cigarettes.

'C'mon.'

Slamming the drawer shut in disgust, he heads out the front door without waiting for me.

'Gonna give it a miss,' I say. Can't get over how weak my voice sounds when I stand up to Jakey.

'Whaa?' He spins round, head jutting forward on his neck, and I have to change my mind. Get to my feet.

'Naa, don't bother,' he says by the time I've got my jacket on. 'Sean 'n' Waz are sick of your coupon. See y'later if I need to crash.'

Sammy Orr was our sergeant. Thirty-odd, we thought he was ancient. Wise, was Sammy. We all looked up to him. You'd laugh at me saying that if you saw him. He was the shortest man among us with yon stocky, stumpy build of a fighter. One of those blokes who walk with their fists clenched stiff like they're primed for a punch-up. You came across a few like that in the forces – wee men that have to look as if they're up for it. Usually find they've a chip on their shoulder, but in Sammy's case, appearances couldnae be more wrong. He'd nothing to prove. He was gentle, thoughtful, smart. Went in with his heart, never his fists.

The first to speak up if there was injustice.

The first of us to die.

See, Sammy didnae like the look of Big Taff Murray. He'd not been right for weeks. Dysentery, like the rest of us lived with on and off, only Taff was in a real bad way. And he wasnae breathing right, all his joints swollen. Me and the rest of his mates in the hut were tending Taff through the night while he fought off sweats and rigors. I'd never seen anything afore like the state of Taff; teeth chattering, body thrashing about, eyes staring through us all, not knowing us, talking gibberish.

Probably the dry beriberi, Sammy thought. Be a goner if he wasnae seen to. Course we'd nothing to give the man. Barely a sip of water to slake his drouth. Taff was shouting out, seeing things coming out the walls, mad in his sickness. And d'you know what we'd to do? This is what you want to know, Richard.

We'd to stuff a rag in Taff's mouth to shut him up in case Fat Guard wakened. We'd to pin Taff down – a sick man, and here's four of his pals, barely the strength of a kitten between us, forcing the big prop still. Telling him wheesht, did he want us all beaten senseless? Ever held a butterfly, Richard? Felt the wings flutter against your skin? Then you'll know how it felt when Taff was fighting us to be free.

'Enough's enough,' decided Sammy Orr. 'Taff's never fit for digging railway track.' Taff didnae know if he was

in Burma or Blackpool by this stage, so did Sammy
not march off with his fists clenched to tell Fat Guard
what's what?

7
HOME ALONE

I was twitchy when I didn't hear from Jakey two, three days after the puggy business. Worried that he was still pissed with me, I took a donner up the park – me and the twenty Silk Cut my Old Boy was patting all his pockets looking for. It was so wet trying to shelter in the bushes of Jakey's hideout that I heard myself inviting him back to mine before I knew what's good for me. See, I knew the Old Boy would be out later. 'Don't wait up, Danny,' he said before he went out to play his first pub gig with the Rovin' Eyes Reunited. I was well pumped to get the house to myself. No Old Dear nipping my head. Sole control of the remote. The chance to get back in Jakey's good books after the puggy business. *Hey, my place is empty . . .*

Before Jakey arrives I think I'll get myself in the party mood doing something I've *fantasised* about doing for years. I put my speakers in the hall and max the volume for a sing-along-a-Seth and the Skarrs boys. No danger of bangbangbangbang. *Turn that racket down.*

With Grampa living here I've never been truly home alone, and the chance to have Skarrs Live at Hennessys' has always been an ambition of mine.

But here's an odd thing. With my music playing so loud, I can't relax. I'm twitchy,' thinking about what might be going on behind the music. Is someone breaking in? Is Mr Patel rattling the front door to complain? Was that the phone ringing?

Funny how some things you think'll be sweet, turn out pish. Like having Jakey here tonight after all. Should have figured he wouldn't be alone.

Sean's up the stairs and through my Old Dear's clothes like a ferret on Viagra, pulling out the underwear she hasn't taken with her. It's a hoot at first, seeing Sean mince about in a green Wonderbra, but when he strips off and climbs into my folks' bed, kidding on he's the pair of them, complete with sound effects – I won't spell it out – I want him to stop.

I keep thinking – no, I keep hoping – that any second now I'll hear bangbangbang and Sean'll shut up.

Before I can stop Jakey, he's in Grampa's room.

Saying he can smell piss, sniffing the mattress. He's forcing open Grampa's locked bedside cabinet.

'Key, Danny? Might be money stashed in here.'

I don't want Jakey to burst the cabinet, but you never tell him he can't do anything, because then he'll definitely do it. You have to divert him.

'Och, Jakey, there'll be money downstairs.'

My Old Dear always kept two tenners under a plant pot in the kitchen. Of course there's diddly-squat when I look tonight. Jakey smashes the plant pot against a radiator to make sure.

They don't stay long after that. Jakey pokes about, looking for drink, until I dig out the whisky and gin left over from Grampa's funeral. Sean tries on more of my Old Dear's underwear, and Waz breaks a string on my Old Boy's mandolin.

I wish Jakey and Waz and Sean had never come. I want them to leave because they're mucking up the air quality in my house, and I feel I can't breathe. If Grampa Dan was alive, they'd never have been over the door. My folks would still be here, fighting their Cold War.

'Old Boy's coming back at eleven,' I lie, eventually. 'You guys take the bevvy up the park.'

* * *

I don't know what's worse now: having Jakey and co.
here, or being home alone after all. When Jakey leaves,
I put all the lights out. Sit downstairs, wrapped in a
blanket, wishing the Old Boy would come back soon.
Imagine that? I daren't even put the telly on, in case
Jakey sees the blue screen flickering when he looks
through the blinds.

So my big night in doesn't exactly work out, does it?
I don't even get to sleep it away for interruptions.

My Old Boy phones. Close to midnight. Dozy, I
hardly recognise his voice; slurred and faraway,
shouting over background music. Cheerful singing. A
woman's laughter.

'Ssssh, you lot. Danny? Listen, I'm waiting for
another band to come on. Going to Davy's for a wee jar
after. So if I'm not back, Danny, don't worry . . . Listen,
I'm losing the signal down here . . .'

'Mum phoned –' I begin, but the Old Boy's line was
already dead.

Later – and I'm lying wide awake this time –
Jakey comes back. He rings the bell and bangs the
door at the same time, mindless of the hour. That, in

normal circumstances, my Old Boy would be in.

'Open up, Danny. C'mon.'

He smacks the lounge window with both palms, leaving splayed prints on the glass.

Mr Patel next door tries to chase him. 'Who you want in there? You make breach of the peace. Salma, call the police.'

He gets a mouthful of Skarrs for his trouble:

> *Why don't you go back*
> *To your own land*
> *To your mud huts*
> *And your hovels?*

I nearly let Jakey in to make him stop. His voice echoes through our cul-de-sac, giving Mr Patel all this racist crap about stinking the neighbourhood out with curry.

'Police?' Jakey shouts. 'They're not gonna come out for tintos.'

'Shut up, shut up, shut up,' I put my fingers in my ears and whisper, willing Jakey to leave. He does, eventually, but only after a scuffle with the new kickboxing couple two doors down.

Cold and uncomfortable on the sofa, I watch night lift through a chink in the curtains, remembering how Mrs Patel used to pick me and Richard up from primary school every day with Ali, her daughter.

At some point I drop off, although it's one of those sleeps where you think you're awake all the time.

'Danny!!'

RatatatTAT.

There's only one person apart from myself who knocks like that.

It was code so our folks didn't need to answer the door.

That'll be Richard for you, Danny.

I only open my door a smidgin, in case the Patels are spying. But there's no movement from their house. Richard looks worried.

'You're all right, Danny?'

Richard's voice is as anxious as his face. He's peeking round the crack I've made, checking me out in my blanket. I'm probably not looking my best.

'I phoned last night.'

'Did you?'

With some folk you can get away with kidmaleery, as Grampa would say. Not with Richard.

'You know fine, Danny.'

We eyeball each other pretty hard for a few seconds, and believe it or not I feel myself reddening under Richard's stare. Flustered, I let him in.

'Heard about your mum leaving,' Richard says, when he's standing in the hall. 'That's why I phoned. Must be rough.'

Richard's clocking the state of the house while we're talking – trying not to be obvious about it, though it's obvious to me.

'They never did decorate,' I hear myself apologising. This was a standing joke between Richard and myself. When we first moved in, my Old Boy stripped the disgusting swirly brown-and-yellow hall wallpaper, but only as far as his ladder would reach. The upper third remained swirly brown. Then my Old Dear started bringing home wallpaper samples, sticking them on the stripped walls to see which ones would grow on her. Later she switched to match pots instead. Used to let me and Richard slosh them up, only he sloshed and I painted: animals, faces, patterns . . .

'Your designs knock the spots off anything I've seen down B&Q, Danny,' she'd say.

Ten years on it's all still there. Tatty, curling scraps of clashing colour. *Richard and Danny. Danny and Richard. Rule OK.*

People don't redecorate during a Cold War.

Just like old times, Richard and I wander into the kitchen first.

Hi, Mrs Hennessy.

Hi, Richard.

I wish we hadn't bothered, the kitchen being in even more of a state than the hall. Decorated, mind, Jakey's dried-in footprints like avant-garde stencils on the units.

'Jeez,' I hear Richard exhale at my back.

'Servant left,' I joke, nonchalant, but seeing the state of this place through someone else's eyes is as much of a shock for me as it must be for Richard.

'Your dad still in bed?' asks Richard.

'Don't think he's in. I'll check.'

Any excuse to get out of the kitchen, I trudge upstairs, Richard in tow. His presence, frankly, is disconcerting. It's a long time since I had a shadow.

'Don't you have rugby on a Saturday?' I say, pointedly. *Take a hint, Richard. Leave me alone.*

That's what part of me's thinking, peeved that Richard still feels we're chummy enough for him to check up on me. But I'm even more peeved at myself. Annoyed at how pleased I am to see him. He carries with him years and years of good memories that I've locked away somewhere. Memories that have never been matched since we stopped being pals. This sounds cringy, but there's something in my chest unfurling, threatening to reach out to Richard, and I'm scared of what'll happen if it does.

'Quit rugby,' he says. 'I'm free on Saturdays now.'

We're paused on the landing, outside Grampa Dan's room.

'How you going to get on without him, Danny?'

No one but Richard would ask a question like that though he doesn't even give me a chance to answer. '*I miss him,*' he says. 'Would it be OK to have a minute in his room?'

Richard takes so long upstairs that, believe it or not, I make a start on the kitchen. Not by choice. Went to make us both a cuppa, but all the mugs were manky. So I wash one and keep going.

After all my hard work Richard doesn't even come down for the tea I've made and Grampa's door is closed when I pass on my way to get dressed. 'Still in there?' I call, because I can't think of anything better. 'You can go now,' being a tad obvious.

Truth is, I don't really want Richard to leave, even though I don't know how to deal with him being here, either. There's something about his presence reminding me of Grampa Dan being here whenever I came home.

'What you doing, Richard?'

I call through from my room now, pulling on yesterday's clothes.

'Looking at this picture,' Richard says, his voice drowned as 'Torture', Skarr's thrashing debut single, pumps the house:

> *With overpopulation*
> *You'll always get starvation*
> *You gotta cull not multiply*
> *Each generation, the weak must DIE.*

Headbanging, I make sure the sound's loud enough to hear through in Grampa Dan's room.

'You don't like that drivel, do you?' Richard shouts. When I burst, air-guitaring, through Grampa's door, he's curling his lip *à la* my Old Dear, shaking his head at the picture he's holding in both hands.

'Don't be a jessie,' I mutter, hoping Richard can't lipread.

'What?' he shouts back, pointing at his ears.

'Brilliant, yeah?' I yell, and join Seth for the stonking chorus:

> *You and you and you should never be here;*
> *You and you and you should be dead.*
> *You and you and you are too sickly;*
> *You don't de-serve to be fed.*

'Great start to the day,' I tell Richard when I've turned the music down a bit.

'How can you like that stuff? Lyrics are outrageous.'

'OOOH!!! Out-RAGE-ous, matron.' I sound like Jakey. 'They're brilliant,' I add in my own voice.

'Aye right, Danny,' Richard mumbles, so flat, so quiet that I can hardly hear him. His cheeks, I notice, still flush like two red Giant Smarties when something about me pisses him off.

'I hope your Grampa never heard that garbage, did he?' Richard sets down the picture, adjusting the way it's sitting on Grampa Dan's bedside table.

I turn it round to face me and bend down to look at it. 'Skarrs are mega.'

'Their lyrics are an insult to his memory, Danny.' Richard speaks quietly, frowning into the tiny watercolour of a matchstick-thin man wearing a pair of raggy shorts. The figure stands under an oversized orange sun with his arms held high in the air, supporting a thick, heavy-looking branch. There's faded writing along the bottom of the frame.

Punishment for sleeping on duty.
36 hours.
Burma 1943.
By Corporal D. Hennessy.

Lighten up, Richard, I'm thinking. It's only music.

Sammy wasnae back from Fat Guard's hut when we set off for another day's labour, clearing path for the Japs' bloody railway. Tom Merry was put out, I remember: he'd have volunteered to stay behind and wipe Taff's arse if it meant a day off digging like Sammy must have wangled. I let him grumble. Said nothing. But I knew. In my water. Something wasnae right.

Mid-morning, Fat Guard marched Sammy out to where the rest of us worked, a rope tight round his neck. Had him standing to attention beside us till night fell, two sentries posted at his back. Bayonets drawn.

Sammy faced us, arms held high over his head. He'd taken some beating, because his eyes were swollen shut, and the flies were swarming over his face. You wanted to look at him, Richard, see how he was doing, but the minute you raised your own eyes from the earth you were digging, Fat Guard himself brought the butt of his stick down on your neck. Again. And again. *'No stop. Twice hard today. Speedo. Speedo. Two man short.'*

All day standing was Sammy. Insects in his eyes and mouth and ears, feeding on his blood, and him not able to move his arms and swipe them off. He was bareheaded, shirtless, nothing on him but an excuse of a pair of shorts. Burning up, he must have been. Sun moving round his body like a blowtorch. When it settled behind him it threw his shadow on the ground in the shape of a cross.

Mind when Jesus is in the Garden of Gethsemane, Richard? Scared to death, wishing he didnae have to die but he knows there's no way out. His card's marked, his cross staring him in the face. He asks the apostles to stay awake with him, keep him company.

But they let him down. So he faces his darkest hour alone.

Us blokes digging? We were like the apostles; too scared of Fat Guard to look up at our suffering pal.

But we were all praying, I suppose. Especially when we realised why Taff – who could barely lift his shovel – was digging a hole behind Sammy.

8
SOUL FOOD

You'll be thinking I'm a hypocrite: accepting Richard's invitation back to his place while we're up in Grampa Dan's room, then spending the first morning in nearly four years catching up with him. Well, it's not that we ever fell out as such. Just drifted apart. He's still OK, although clearly we don't have a million things in common like we used to. He's into crap music for a start, dreepy depressing mope-in-your-bedroom-and-slit-your-wrists singer-songwriter stuff. Difficult not to judge him on that, especially when he criticised me about Skarrs.

Still, he ascends several rungs in my estimation when he asks me if I've had breakfast then proceeds to cook this uber-fry-up: bacon, eggs, potato scones, black pudding. Mega! Haven't eaten anything as good since my Old Dear's last chilli.

Richard's phone rings non-stop while he cooks. I'm

left hanging around like a bad smell, eavesdropping.

'Nah. Can't this morning, Colin. Someone's here. No . . . not *her*. Danny. Old mate from primary. No. You won't know him.'

'Joe! Yeah, done the history. Found a website. Phone you tomorrow?'

His final call comes while we're eating.

'Hiya. No. My folks are out for the day. *All* day. *And* later. *Very* good idea . . . Hour or so? Just having breakfast.'

'That a burd,' I ask with a knowing wink although I know fine it is by the way Richard's voice has changed.

'Yeah, you know her, Danny,' he says, demolishing the last piece of toast. Licking his fingers. Not a flinch of embarrassment.

Then he riles me.

'D'you think your mum'll come back?'

We were running out of small talk by this stage. Between phone calls Richard brought me up to speed with himself:

He still plays piano.

And he's first trumpet in the school orchestra.

Striker in the football team.

Member of the local badminton club.

He'll do five Highers.

Take a gap year travelling.

Study history and economics at Uni.

All mapped out.

'What about you, Danny? Still mad keen on art? Remember you used to carry your wee sketchbook everywhere . . .?'

That's when our conversation peters – or Dannys – out.

What am *I* going to do? I can only tell Richard what I won't be doing: five Highers and going to Uni the way things are panning out. The thought turns my breakfast sour in my stomach. In a long silence, broken by slurps of tea, Richard asks about the Old Dear.

Do I think she'll come back?

The million-dollar question; I didn't even know she was going away.

'Dunno.'

'Must be tough without her, Danny.'

'Yeah. Boohoo.'

I don't want Richard looking at me the way he's looking at me so I take my plate to the bin and scrape it, even though I've licked the pattern off it.

My tongue feels as though it could easily start talking about things, but my brain won't let it. It's that unfurling sensation in my chest again. I feel my head reining back feelings that I daren't turn into words. Don't know what might come out if I begin.

'Look, Danny, you know if you want to talk –' Richard starts, not sounding any way near as cheesy as it must look on paper.

'I'm fine,' I say, heading for the front door. 'Thanks for the grub.'

Richard's not giving up.

'Danny, I'm around later. Fancy a video? A pizza? Mum and Dad are away till late –'

'Nah. Doin' something.'

I'm already squeezing out Richard's front door. In a bit of a hurry now. What would Jakey have to say if he knew I was being tempted to sit in on a Saturday night watching videos with Dicky-Head?

'I'll be in touch, Danny,' Richard calls after me. 'I've stuff to tell you about Grampa Dan.'

I don't get the chance to ask him what he means because this burd breezes past me on Richard's path.

What a filthy look she gives me. Can hardly blame her.

It's Ali Patel.

9
MUMMY'S HOME

I stare at Richard's front door long after Ali's disappeared behind it. *What's going . . . ? Why would she . . . ? Not with Richard, surely?* My head's muttering away to itself while my hand stabs randomly with my key at my own front door. Which is open already, I realise. When I nearly poke my Old Dear's eye out. Bizarrely, she's wearing her outdoor coat with a pair of pink rubber gloves. She never wears rubber gloves. Family germs won't kill me, she used to say, even if I puked up all over the shop.

'Danny. Where've you been?'

What a cheek my Old Dear's got. Where have *I* been?

'Out,' I snap, breenging past her up to my room, although my heart's going like the clappers at the sight of her. I shut my door and lean against it.

Man, I'm angry. But I'm shaking, and I can't figure out why.

I mean, she's a *complete* pain, my Old Dear. On my

back twenty-four seven, her and her verbal GBH.

Is that lager on your breath?

You've been smoking.

You're late!

Then out of the blue, she buggers off, taking her nagging with her. And I'm even madder with her. How dare she! She's thirty-eight. Ancient. Supposed to be predictable.

'Danny.'

She's tapping my door with her nails. Speaking soft. Not angry.

'Where's Dad?'

'Out. Duh! Told you last night.'

'Out where, Danny?' She's struggling to keep a lid on her exasperation. Being 'nice'.

'Dunno.'

It's magic when you draw things out like this, or as Seth says:

> *Squirm, squirm*
> *Little worm*
> *Writhe and suffer*
> *Squirm, squirm*

'When did your father go out, Danny?'

'Dunno. Seven, half seven.'

'So early?'

'Last night.' *Squirm, squirm.*

'Last night? He left you on your own?'

'I'm fifteen,' I remind her. Come on, I'm hardly going to let on how much I hated being home alone.

'Shouldn't have left you.' She lets out a big sigh.

'Who? He shouldn't or *you* shouldn't,' I say. Then I get the music on and blare her out of earshot:

Squirm, squirm
Little worm
Red and slick
On my stick.
Squirm, squirm
Little worm.

Soon as my Old Boy does come home, all hell breaks loose downstairs. The racket wakes me up. After my lousy night on the sofa, I'd turned my music off and drifted into sleep, listening to all the domestic sounds of my Old Dear at work downstairs. Today, familiar sounds are so . . . so . . . I know, how can I say hoovering's soothing? But that's what it felt like. Sent me off into a dream. Behind all the other sounds was the rumble of the washing machine: the swooshing as the drum filled, then the thrum of its slow heavy circles. Something about the washing machine noise made me think I was listening to the engine of a boat. The Millport ferry to be precise.

We used to go to Millport – this wee holiday island – in long weekends. In the days when Grampa would let a relief nurse come in. We'd ride the train from Glasgow to Largs, then sail the fifteen-minute boat crossing to Millport. There, we'd hire out bikes and cycle round the island. Ten miles, nearly all flat. Last time we went, I was just big enough to share a tandem with my Old Boy. We were so uncoordinated that the Old Dear lost the rag with us and cycled off on her own.

I'm dreaming that I'm cycling after her on my tandem. I'm calling her, waving a drawing I've done for her, but she's ignoring me.

'Wait . . .' my voice croaks in sleep when the front door slams and the rammy downstairs wakens me. From my window I see Mr Patel leaving our house. Mrs Patel's waiting at the door for him.

She must be able to hear my Old Dear shouting at the Old Boy. Of course, he never shouts back. Only the occasional rumble of his voice when he manages to get a word in edgewise betrays his presence. Surprise, surprise, my name crops up a few times, my Old Dear demanding to know why 'that ned Jakey Wilson's been over my door?'

Rumble, rumble, rumble.

That's probably what my Old Boy actually says. *I* would. No point in arguing with my Old Dear when she's on a roll, managing to fit my truanting, drinking, wearing the same underpants till they stand up by themselves, and all my Old Boy's shortcomings into one nag. I tell you, she'd make a wicked rapper if she was twenty years younger.

You've nothing to say to him.

Good or bad.

You don't set limits.

You don't advise.

You let him do what the hell he likes.

And sit there strumming your life away.

Chorus:

No wonder your son is outa control.

I don't wait for the second verse. Heard – and *taken* – the Danny Rap a million times. Instead I take advantage of my Old Dear's Missy Elliot-esque solo to dip my Old Boy's jacket pocket.

Stuff them both.

Twenty quid up, at least I know Jakey'll be pleased to see me for once.

10
ALI PATEL

I don't recall instructing my legs to take a detour down Richard's path, but they do it anyway. I'm kidding myself this has nothing to do with wanting to know the score with him and Ali Patel, but while I wait for Richard to answer the door I try to see through his front-room window.

Green eyes. Ali Patel has green eyes. And jet-black hair cropped so short it spikes up in all directions, the way I could never do mine. Skin that looks tanned, even in winter, and a laugh that sounds better than the chorus of your favourite song. She taught me and Richard to skateboard on the ramp she built in front of her house.

'You took your time.'

I can't disguise the suspicion in my voice when Richard appears. And I'm doing what he did when he came to my door earlier, only I'm not clocking the state of his wallpaper. I'm more interested in the state of Ali Patel. I can see her in the mirror over Richard's shoulder. He can't know it reflects into his lounge. Neither can Ali Patel, otherwise I doubt she'd be footering quite so unselfconsciously with all those straps at her shoulders, smoothing down a wee black vest that's ridden up over her stomach. Last time I saw her so dishevelled, she was flat on the pavement with her face up the exhaust of Mr Patel's car because she'd taken her grindpole too fast.

'Danny!'

Richard's looking a bit more crumpled than normal himself. Breathless; two wee red activity spots on each cheek. I have to give it to him though; he's a cool customer, switching from Mr Lover-Lover to Friends Reunited without batting an eyelid.

'C'mon in. Remember Ali?'

Ali's less adaptable. Embarrassed, maybe, at getting caught in the middle of – what would Jakey call it? – a spot of rumpy-pumpy. Annoyed, more probably, at having to exchange social niceties with the likes of me.

One night last summer, Jakey, Waz, Sean and myself met Ali Patel. She was playing tennis in the park with her cousin, Jay, who used to skateboard with me sometimes. Jakey shoved us close against the fence round the courts to watch them.

'It's like seeing the gorillas in the zoo,' Jakey megaphoned.

'What you staring at, bhoona-breaths?' he challenged, when Ali and Jay glared over. 'Sorry. Havenae brought you any bananas the day.'

Waz and Sean appreciated Jakey's wisecrack so much they leapt up on the court fence and clung to it like a pair of gorillas themselves. They used their weight to rock the fence until the wires broke loose from one of the posts holding it up and it started to collapse into the court. All the time they threw in the best racist insults they could scrape together:

'Hey mate, you've got dirty legs.'

'Who's lookin' after the shop while you're here?'

'Anyone for curry?'

To be honest, at first I wasn't really paying attention to the situation. Jakey, Waz and Sean have a go at anyone they don't like the look of, or anyone who's doing anything that looks gay. They make a particular effort to pick on our 'brothers and sisters from diverse racial backgrounds', as Gubby might say. I tend to stay out of things until it gets to the point where I *have* to join in or risk getting turned on by Jakey myself.

When I saw Ali Patel on the tennis court, I heard all Jakey's racist crap loud and clear, but it was like it had nothing to do with me, really. Or Ali. See, I was concentrating on her legs, thinking she didn't have skateboarding scabs down her shins any more, and I used to think they were cool. Now her legs were doing something weird to my insides. They were perfect; not thin, or twiggy. (Hate burds with skinny legs; that's more Jakey's taste for you.) There was muscle definition on Ali Patel's legs. They weren't long legs either, but neat and strong, and they looked awesome against the baggy white shorts she was wearing. The rest of her was haggard too. White T-shirt, not quite long enough to hide the cheeky wee wink of her belly-button ring when she stretched up for a ball.

Not that she hit many more balls once we arrived. She tried to keep the game going, beckoning Jay up to the net and forming a 'wee brown huddle', as Jakey sneered in his Indian accent.

But we'd got to them bigtime. They were mucking up

every shot and when we pointed and made chimp noises they played even worse. That was when Ali Patel lost the place and fired a ball at the fence.

After the names Jakey called her and the suggestions he made while Waz and Sean doofed Jay's belly with his own racket, I can't blame Ali Patel for looking at me now like I'm snot.

'Oh, I remember Danny.' Ali says my name as if it tastes bad. 'Pity you weren't around yesterday evening when your Nazi pal was insulting my dad.'

Her green eyes won't meet mine, but I know that she knows that I know that she knows I was in when Jakey noised up her Old Man last night.

Here's my chance to get back on a civil footing with Ali Patel.

Sorry, I could say. *All that stuff's got nothing to do with me. You know I'm not racist. Man, I fancy you rotten.*

Unfortunately, I don't do sorry. Apologies stick in my craw.

'What're you on about?' I say to Ali Patel, and I borrow the curdling look Jakey uses when he wants to give one burd the heave and ensure she doesn't think he's just playing hard to get.

The bitterness in my tone corrodes my throat like acid, but I can't go back on myself, can I?

'Are you coming in, Danny?'

I'm guessing that Richard doesn't know about the tennis court business or the hassle last night, else he wouldn't still be trying to steer me inside, all palsy-walsy. 'We're phoning for a pizza now. Fancy staying?'

It's difficult to convey quite how pleased Richard seems to be that I'm here, grinning from ear to ear, *totally* oblivious to Ali Patel's stormy glower.

'This is a reunion,' he beams. 'We'll have the ramp out in the street next.'

You don't know me that well yet, so I should tell you: I can be right thrawn. Driven by this urge to do exactly the opposite of what 'nice' people want, just to see the disappointment in their faces. Gives me this feeling, not of pleasure exactly, but of power, I suppose. A buzz. A rush.

So when I look at Richard as if he's a bit Dolly Dimple and say with distain, 'Nah, I'm meeting my mates tonight,' it feels good when I see his big grin drop. But then I have to make a readjustment. I can be a bad bugger.

You see, while Richard's looking glum that I'm

leaving, I notice Ali Patel's shoulders relaxing in a sigh of relief.

'But I'll come back round later,' I beam, all chipper. Just to make her night.

Some friends we were, eh?, Scared to look at Taff while he kept digging out that hole. By dark it wasn't deep enough, so when the guards changed shift, the ones going off duty shoved Taff out the road so they could finish the job quickstyle. They laughed when they bent over Taff, poking him with their bayonets like I used to prod a crab at the seaside when I was a boy to see if it was still alive. If they'd only looked where Taff's skin dipped under his ribs they'd have seen his heart fluttering.

Fat Guard made us stand in a semi-circle, then swung Sammy Orr round to face us. The hole Taff had dug separated us from him, and I don't know if Sammy could see us. His hands were still clasped above his head.

Fat Guard ordered us all to move back a bit while he took a few practice swings in the air with his rifle. You'd think the bastard was going out to bat on the bloody cricket field, the way he swaggered behind

Sammy and – whack – caught him a belter round the back of the knees.

Not a sound came from Sammy as his legs buckled, taking him into Taff's hole.

What d'you think came next?

I don't know if I can tell you.

I don't know if I can say.

But this is what you were wanting to hear.

And this is what you have to tell Danny for me.

11
WITH FRIENDS LIKE THESE . . .

'Hall-o. It's the Sleepin' Beauty.'

I haven't spoken to Jakey since I didn't let him in last night. When I climb the hill to his den at the top of the park, and an empty bottle clips my ear before it smashes on the path, it dawns that I'd have been wiser body swerving him for a few days more.

'Better keep your hearing aid switched on the night for me, Danny-Boy.' At least Jakey's laughing.

I kid on I'm daft, wear my puzzled face. 'What you on about, Jakey?'

'You sayin' you didnae hear me, Danny-boy? Christ, the whole of Little India was out in the street.'

'Never heard a thing. I was knackered.' I can't look at Jakey when I lie. Busy myself offering round fags, courtesy of my Old Boy's money. Jakey's eyes bore my forehead and I try to keep the flame steady on my lighter. Waz and Sean are staring too. They blow hot and cold with me: one nod from Jakey and they'd turn in a flash.

'Better not be sleeping next time I drop in, Danny-Boy.'

Jakey gives me that grin that doesn't match the look in his eyes, or the threat in his voice. 'Else you'll really be knackered.'

With friends like these, eh? you must be thinking. Why would any self-respecting guy put up with a mate who treats him like Jakey treats me?

Well, in Jakey's defence I can only say that he treats everyone the same. Because he's a one-off, he says. And because I hang out with him, that makes me a one-off too. I like that.

Jakey says him and me and Waz and Sean are mates because we go our own way. That's why we're into Skarrs instead of all the naff MTV drivel everyone else listens to. He likes to take the credit for turning us on to Skarrs, forgetting that it was actually *me* who discovered them. Listened to my Old Dear sounding off about an article on this band who'd been dropped by their record label because their lyrics had incited some white kids to shoot up a black school in America. Just as well none of their poison can be released in Britain, she said, so of course I got busy and downloaded everything I could on Skarrs. I *knew* Jakey would be impressed, although it took a few listens before any of us got into the music properly. Seth Lamprey scream-sings to be heard over the feedback, and none of the guitars are tuned up together. Deliberate, of course. Like no other band. And Seth's lyrics, they're so in your face they make the Beatles look like zeroes and the Stones a shower of limp nancies. So Jakey thinks. I've imported every demo, bootleg and delete Skarrs have recorded and I burn copies for the others. No one else I know is into Skarrs. That's why I'm surprised Richard knew anything about them.

Richard. Like that Kylie song I should be ashamed to know the chorus to, I can't get him out of my head tonight. Him and Ali Patel. La la lying on his sofa.

Ha, Richard, at least you don't know anything about being up here; highest point of the park. Top of the world, Ma! Where it feels like me and Jakey and Waz and Sean really are different from everyone else.

Because this is where we don't just talk about what we're gonna do, Jakey says. This is where we do it.

Jakey says you're really only out of your box if you don't remember. If you wake up and haven't a scoobie where you are, who you are, what you've done. That's really doing it, he says. That's why *we're* different.

Like a lot of things about Jakey, his just-do-it philosophy scares me. See, he's mental. So are the others. Up for trying anything going. Waz'll drink till he blacks out. Sean mixes booze and pills. Any pills. He's had fits. Once we'd to dump him at casualty and run.

Me? I only like booze – not even the taste, just the feeling of being slightly out of it, though not so I don't know what's what. A few times I've gone over the score and, to be honest, the puking and headache that comes with a bender are enough to keep me away from Jakey and the bevvy until he comes looking for me.

As for drugs, I'm just not into them.

That's my Achilles heel with Jakey and co. I'll kid on I'm trying whatever's going. Pop the pill. Have a smoke. But I never swallow, and I don't inhale. I watch to see how the other three react and I do the same with knobs on. Roll about moaning, dance like a drongo, stare into space until the others fall asleep and I slip off home.

So far I've got away with it.

What worries me is when one of the guys brings gear that needs a needle, or cooking up. Till now it's mainly been parents' bathroom cupboard stuff: uppers, downers, sleeping pills, Grampa Dan's laxatives once – BIG mistake – or whatever Jakey scrounges from Nut, the bampot brother who's meant to be looking after him. Lately though, Jakey's been boasting about buying from a real dealer. Scares the crap out of me.

'Gotta try it, to deny it, Danny-Boy,' Jakey says.

The way he looks at me, sly, half smiling, I'm sure he's got me sussed.

Thankfully it's only booze tonight, courtesy of Waz and Sean. Jakey wants to know what I've brought. 'Just fags, Danny-Boy?'

He trousers the change from my twenty quid and turns away.

Nobody's talking to me. It's always like that when I arrive last.

They're lying on the grass, passing a bottle between them, squinting up at me through smoke from the cigarettes I've lit for them. Nobody offers me a drink and

I don't like to sit down without an invitation. There's a wee power game going on. Jakey gets a buzz making one of us feel awkward. Likes to keep us on our toes.

And, man, it works. 'Anything happening?' I ask at last, to break the ice.

'What's it look like, Danny-Boy,' Jakey replies after a long pause, blowing a puff of smoke into my eyes.

'*Anythin' happening?*' Waz and Sean chorus, and they collapse over each other, snorting.

That's when I remember for once I *have*, amazingly, been invited somewhere else tonight. 'Listen, I'll leave you to it,' I say.

I've never done this, dismissed myself without Jakey's say-so. Even when I'm halfway down the hill I expect him to roar me back. *Where the hell you off to, Danny-Boy? You don't have any other mates.* But there's no call.

'Where's that wee sad-case going now?' I hear Waz slur.

'Who gives,' Jakey replies, and I couldn't honestly say if the sigh I give is one of disappointment or relief.

We'd to kneel round the hole and use our hands to shove back the earth that Taff dug out. Pressing it round Sammy's neck like you'd pack topsoil to support a new flower you were planting.

'Pack tight. Pack tight. Speedo!' Fat Guard was screeching at us if we slacked. 'Silence!' if one of us tried to whisper useless comfort in Sammy's ear.

Then we'd to stand back. And watch. And watch. Fat Guard first. Then his sentries. Two of the four joined in. Walked away from Sammy. Fixed their bayonets. Used his eyes for target practice.

Over.

And over.

And we watched.

And we watched.

And all we could do was

nothing.

12
AN EVENING IN THE PARK WITH GRAMPA

It's such a cracking night in the park – close, but not stuffy – that I don't leave for Richard's straight away. Instead I head for the boating pond, where I used to come every evening with my Old Boy on my bike.

'Let's us get out from Mum's feet,' he'd say, 'before she sees us sitting still and makes us do something.'

I'd cycle round and round the pond like a gerbil on a wheel while my Old Boy walked, and I'd be so much faster than he was on foot that I'd have to keep doubling back to meet him.

Tonight I'm hoping the bloke at the boat-hire's gone home. Last time I was here he chased me in his van after Jakey and I threw lighted newspaper into one of the boats and pushed it into the middle of the pond in flames. We were re-creating a Viking burial ceremony. There was a sacrificial duck involved.

I pass the swing park, nearly empty now. At the roundabout a lone sprog strains to make it turn for him. He gets it going a few centimetres, jumps on eagerly, and it stops.

'Jump on. I'll spin,' I offer, since I'm passing. Tugging the bar for him, I ask, 'Is that fast enough? D'you want faster?'

The wee sprog doesn't seem too comfortable having a stranger pushing him. He's peering beyond me anxiously, and when each slowing revolution of the roundabout brings him back to me, he whimpers.

Footsteps approach and this plump bloke's beside me. I think I recognise him from somewhere, though I can't quite place him. No stranger to a jam doughnut, he's carrying a toddler with one of those press-my-tummy chuckles under his arm. A baby sprog, dangling from a sling contraption on Plump Bloke's chest, stares me out.

'You getting a birl, Gordy?' Plump Bloke calls to Mister Anxious on the roundabout, who responds by trying to dive off the thing while it's still moving. Plump Bloke and I both lunge together to stop the kid from taking a header, but I get there first, setting Mister

Anxious on his feet while Plump Bloke untangles the baby who's tumbled his wilkies in the sling.

I've really scared the life out of Mister Anxious now. He's gawping at me through Plump Bloke's knees as if I've got two spinning heads on the end of my neck. Expecting at least a glare of irritation from Plump Bloke for inducing roundabout phobia in his son, I sidle a few steps towards the park exit when I'm stopped in my tracks.

'What's the matter, Gordy? You not saying thanks to Danny for pushing you?'

It's the voice that jogs my memory first, not the fact that Plump Bloke's used my name. *I* know where I've seen him before, though it was weeks ago now, through a looping hangover.

'Grampa Dan says your hair's much better, now it's growing back in, Danny. You're a bloody mess otherwise,' says Mister Derek.

I'm hearing things. Must be hearing things. Mister Derek's words even have me looking over my shoulder to see if he's talking to someone else. But no, he's holding my gaze with those blue eyes that I remember now I see them again. He's smiling at me, not in the least fazed that I'm responsible for the wreck of a child clinging to his legs.

I'm too gobsmacked to get my voice working until Mister Derek's scooped up Mister Anxious and walked away. He's singing 'Time to Go Home' – Old Dear and I used to sing the same song together, cooried up at the end of my *Watch With Mother* video – the sprog in the crook of his arm clobbering him on the face and bawling, 'No.' By the time I catch up with him, the baby in the sling's crying too.

'How d'you know about me?' I shout over the sprog chorus, sending Mister Anxious into paroxysms of sobbing. Mister Derek beams through the misery.

'Grampa Dan's talking to me, Danny. He says you have to speak to Richard.'

And he's off, bouncing cheerfully across the grass as if his weans are all singing 'It's a Wonderful World' instead of greeting their heads off. As I contemplate running after him, he turns and waves at me with his free arm. Yells:

'I have to go now. But remember: Richard can help you.'

13
JUST LIKE OLD TIMES

'I'll bloody speak to Richard all right,' I mutter as I storm up his path. Find out exactly what HE's got to do with MY Grampa. I thump his front door with my fist.

'Danny.' No welcome grin this time, alas. No eye contact. Richard doesn't disguise the chill in his voice. Ali Patel's been talking. And you know what? Richard's air of disapproval brings out the worst in me.

'What film d'you get? Smut 'n' gore, I hope.'

I squeeze past Richard and take myself into his front room – empty – making a pantomime of kicking off my trainers, getting comfy on the settee, plumping up a squashed cushion at my back. I catch a whiff of perfume from it.

'We've not done this for a while,' I say, acting oblivious to the bad vibes. He hovers just inside the room, arms folded across his chest, chewing away at his lip.

'Ali gone for the pizzas?'

'She's away home.'

'Oh.' I pretend to pat around for the remote control. 'Only you and me, then: just like old times.'

There's a silence. A long one. I can practically hear Richard picking his words before he says, 'Ali didn't want to be here in case you came back.'

'Three's a crowd, eh?' I try not to squirm, adding, 'What are burds like,' sounding as if I know, although the closest I get to anything female is if some old granny rubs up beside me on the bus.

'Ali told me about you and your mates at the tennis. How could you do that, Danny?'

'Och,' I begin to say, 'a joke. I never joined in –' but Richard interrupts: 'What's happened to you? You're in a right mess.'

He leaves the room, his opinion – no. Not just his opinion. Grampa Dan's, too – swirling round me, clawing at my rumbling belly.

What am I doing here anyway? What would Jakey say if he saw me? Who needs Richard, I think, letting myself out. Can't be thinking straight. Probably malnutrition. Apart from Richard's fry-up I haven't had one decent meal since the Old Dear legged it. Can't be healthy, living on chips and carry-outs ever since . . . ever since . . .

'Since you died,' I whisper, looking up at Grampa Dan's blank window from the doorstep of my own house. It's in darkness and I know by the hollow rattle of the key in the lock that nobody's home. A pang of hunger swoops from my brain to my belly, so powerful that I have to clutch myself to keep standing. I'm overwhelmed by silence rushing me from all the empty rooms.

There's an old echo in my head: 'Hiya, Grampa! It's me.'

Bang Bang Bang.

I'd be dead meat if Jakey clocked me now, shifting from one foot to the other, waiting for Richard to answer his door. But I just can't face being alone again in my house.

There were notes, you see, one from each of them.

Old Dear's was in an envelope. Sealed. Left on my pillow:

> Danny,
>
> I really need to talk to you. Wish you hadn't gone out tonight without saying. I'll be collecting you from school on Monday. New mobile number below. Don't give it to your dad.
>
> Love you,
>
> Mum

Old Boy's was scrawled across a page torn from the phone book:

> Gig. Airdrie – Flares. Back late. Lock up.

'Danny.'

Not you again, sigh Richard's upturned eyes when he finds me on his doorstep. I steel myself.

'Fancy coming round to mine instead?'

I know. Should be kicking off with *Sorry, Richard,* but as I've explained: I don't do sorry.

Instead I make my invitation sound as though I'm doing Richard a favour. And he buys it. I knew he would.

'Don't blame you wanting company,' he mind-reads when we go inside my place. I notice he cocks his head to one side, looking up the stairs, and I know who he's listening for.

I don't know what to say to Richard now he's here. It's awkward.

'Toast?' I suggest. By the time it's ready Richard's sneaked up to sit on Grampa Dan's bed and watch the football highlights. Like the pair of them used to do together on a Saturday night.

I'd stand outside Grampa's door listening, wishing I knew what they were on about. Wishing *I* could make Grampa sound so bright. His face would be lit up when I came in, but I always changed the subject.

'Guess what, Grampa? *Goldfinger*'s on the other side. Your favourite Bond song's in it.'

He was *my* Grampa, after all. Why should Richard be the one he confided in? He had me.

He had me, I'm thinking, staring hard at Richard. He changes the channel and picks up Grampa's picture of that matchstick man under the burning sun again, ignoring the plate of toast I put on the mattress beside him. I might be wrong, but I think there are tears in his eyes. For some reason the sight angers me, and I snatch the picture from Richard, setting it on the cabinet Jakey tried to burst open the other night.

My picture. Not yours.

I shoogle at the locked handle.

'Don't, Danny,' says Richard quietly. 'I've got the key to that.'

'Why would Grampa give you the key?' *And not me*, I demand. Raging inside I am.

Give Richard his due. He has the decency to look embarrassed. 'Grampa Dan wanted to tell you things, show you things, but he said you weren't listening to him any more.'

'What?' I'm on my feet now. 'How d'you know this?'

'I taped him. For a history project.'

I know this already, don't I? Old Dear mentioned it at Grampa's funeral. Should have pressed her when I had the chance.

'Where was I when you were taping?'

Richard shrugs. 'Out.'

'When?'

'Evenings, couple of weeks before your Grampa died. D'your mum not say at the time?'

Course, the Old Dear could have said. She said lots of things. Why would I bother to listen, especially if she kicked off with, 'That nice Richard . . .'?

'What would Grampa tell you that he couldn't tell me, anyway? Where he hid his football stickers?'

When I sneer, Richard takes up Grampa's water colour, cradling it.

'Grampa wanted you to know what it was like doing this. He hoped it could teach you something. Thought you would understand because art was something you both –'

'– That's a picture, Richard. How can that teach me anything?'

Richard shakes his head.

'It's what this picture's about, Danny. And other stuff I've to show you. But there's no point in telling you about it till you're ready to listen. Grampa Dan said you'd come to me when it was time –'

Richard's leaving. Hasn't even touched his toast.

'Where's this key then?' I want to know.

'In school with the rest of my project.'

'Bloody cheek. *My* key!'

'Grampa Dan wanted it kept with my tape,' says Richard, already halfway downstairs. 'Said it was a symbol. *Secrets and Scars*. That's what I called my project. Cool title? Grampa Dan thought so.'

Very cool title, I'm thinking, though I say nothing. Scuff the carpet with my toes.

Outside the front door, Richard breaks into one of his ear-splitting grins. 'Grampa Dan got me an A, Danny.'

Bully for you Dicky-Head, I hear Jakey's voice in my head as I manage a weak smile. Shame Grampa Dan can't do anything for my grades.

Fat Guard left Taff for dead along with Sammy and marched us back to camp. Later Mack, Tom Merry, Hopeless and myself slipped out when we thought the coast was clear to try ... I don't know what exactly. Make sure Taff was gone? See what we could do for him? Bring him back? All we knew was we couldnae leave Taff there.

So we're creeping towards the camp boundary, sticking to the shadows, about to slip outside when – Jesus Christ – one of the guards who was there at Sammy's killing leaps out in front of us.

We're done for, I'm thinking. We'd all have been thinking: hands up, huddling together. Me, I'm good for nothing as usual, soiling my shorts, too frightened to breathe let alone think. But Hopeless, he steps forward and points into the dark beyond the camp, turning his pockets inside out then doing this mime of dragging something along the ground. All this and at the same time insisting, 'WE NO ESCAPE. WE BRING BACK FRIEND. LOOK. WE TAKE NOTHING.'

And here's this wee Jap guard – we're all looking down at him, and he's got the point of his bayonet drawing a warning line an inch from my throat. He's one of the guards who threw Taff aside to speedo the digging of Sammy's grave. But not one of the guards who killed him. I sussed that the moment he handed Hopeless his water canteen and stepped aside to let us leave the camp.

When we reached Taff, I whispered he was dead. He was that still, limbs flopping like a rag doll when you moved him. Maybe, I said, we'd be better leaving him be. Save our strength rather than drag his corpse all the way back to camp. Then he groaned. Must've heard.

Jesus. What Taff must've thought, hearing me say 'Leave him' when he was still alive. *Leave him*, spattered in Sammy Orr's blood. *Leave him*. Plagued by the same insects that were feeding on Sammy's corpse. Thinking, so this is where I'm going to die.

Not that conditions were any better once we dragged him back to camp. Still no medicine. The only clean water the drops left in the Jap sentry's canteen. Not one of us was brave enough to face Fat Guard and say,

Help this man. He's dying. Not after Sammy.

Leave him, I said.

Big Taff, who told me, 'Stick by me, Henny, boyo,' at the surrender. Who clamped his arm around me in a bloody vice and held me in line beside him, voice booming so loud that he took a rifle butt across the back of the head. The first act of violence I'd seen in the war. Wood against bone. The noise. *Je-sus.*

My fault, too.

That blow nearly felled Big Taff. He'd swayed, but stayed on his feet, cursing the Japs all the way to the first camp, blood pouring down his neck. I remember thinking that day how he looked chiselled out of granite, like a statue. Forearms like bloody cabers, muscles straining the seams of his shirt. None of us were built like that. That's why you noticed him dwindling more than the others.

When Taff died his eyes were open and his mouth was parted like he was trying to talk. I've had some job convincing myself that he wasnae cursing me for saying 'Leave him'. Because I've heard hearing's the last sense to go . . .

14
DIGGING A HOLE

'Danny is attracted to the disruptive element in this school, Mrs Hennessy, spurning the ethos we strive to foster and uphold.'

You can just tell Gubby loves to flex his polysyllables when he gets the chance. I suppose he's allowed, being an English teacher, and there sure ain't much scope for oratory when he's taking our set, last two on a Friday.

'Danny,' he intones, 'has been afforded countless chances to redeem himself, Mrs Hennessy, to no avail. He's an intelligent boy. With potential . . . flair for language . . . outstanding artistic ability . . . Indeed, Miss West . . . departmental head of art . . . never seen such native talent in a pupil . . .

'Sadly . . . over the years . . . erosion . . . dubious company . . . easily led . . . plummeting self-esteem . . . seems to be digging a hole for himself . . . indicative of problems at home. Perhaps . . . signs of crisis . . .

'In a nutshell, terribly, terribly concerned.'

Blah.

Blah.

Blah.

Heard it all before.

So has the Old Dear. Maybe not quite so eloquently put. This is the first time she's been up in front of Gubby, who's Deputy Head. Recent summonses came from lower down the pep talk tree.

I know what this means. One more strike and it's a Court Martial before the Love Doc, our Head Honcho. After that I'm oot. Like Jakey's brother, Nut, expelled two years ago, after they caught him selling dope to the First Fifteen in the changing room.

Now Gubby's had his say, he waits for my Old Dear to respond, his fingers forming a spindly snooker-type rest for his pointy chin.

But my Old Dear doesn't peep, which is odd. I've never known her stuck for words before. In every previous interview, mind you, my Old Boy's been here to take the bare look of her, keeping shtoom – *told* to keep shtoom – but here none the less.

He wouldn't come today. They'd barneyed big style

on the phone about this meeting with Gubby.

'I know you don't need me, Susan,' my Old Boy had nearly raised his voice to interrupt my Old Dear. 'So there's no point in me turning up, is there?' he finished, cutting her off then phoning in sick to his own school and going back to bed.

My Old Dear never even said a word to me outside Gubby's office while we waited for his green light to enter. Just hugged herself, looking at the floor. None of the usual nip nip nip, *'Now when you go in there, Danny, I want to see a bit of respect and contrition . . .'*

She keeps hugging herself throughout Gubby's speech, like her belly aches. I sneak a look at her. She's done something to her hair, coloured her grey bits goldy maybe, but it doesn't look good because it's hanging straggly on her shoulders, not swinging sharp as her tongue any more. She twists her hands behind Gubby's desk as though she's washing them. *Out, out, damn spot.*

She's not wearing her wedding ring.

'Maybe Danny could give us a few moments, Mrs Hennessy,' says Gubby. He comes round his desk and gestures me outside with a nod.

'Wait there, Danny,' he says, but not strict.

113

As he shuts his door on me I see my Old Dear sink her face into her hands. Part of me – a guilty part? a sad part? Oh, I don't know – wishes I could wreathe invisible back through Gubby's keyhole. Sit beside my Old Dear. Be there for once when she needs me . . .

Out in the corridor, I'm a sitting target for all the filthy *You again, Hennessy* glances from the teachers going in and out of the staffroom. Only Miss West speaks to me. She always speaks to me. Puts her hand on my shoulder. Smiles.

'Life-drawing this afternoon, Danny. Looking forward to seeing how you get on.'

The period bell rings. A gaggle of girls from my registration class pass and ignore me, linked together like paper-chains.

'Is that you getting your parole from this place?'

Jakey, Waz and Sean, strolling in late for first period, form a semi-circle round me, blocking the corridor until Jakey shoves me off my chair with his elbow and takes it himself.

'What you done, Danny-Boy?'

'Nothin'.'

'What you telling Gubby?'

'Nothin'. Old Dear's in.'

'What they doing?'

'Dunno. Talking.'

'What they send you out for? I never get sent out.'

Sean, on tiptoes, squashes his face against the frosted-glass panel of Gubby's door.

'Hey, someone's lying out on Gubby's desk. Your maw wearin' green?'

'Not any more, man.' Waz is jostling for position at the window now, elbowing Sean back.

'Think Gubby's snogging her. Shouldnae have left them alone.'

'Canny blame her, Danny-Boy. She'll be gagging for it with your Old Boy off the scene.'

Jakey grins, although there's no spark of humour across his eyes. His remark is exclusively for my benefit, Waz and Sean too busy shoving each other to hear properly. It's the action of a sadist throwing a stick over the edge of a cliff to relish his daft dog going after it.

That's how he observes me now, hands splayed on his spread thighs, head cocked up at me, waiting to see what I do next. 'Gagging for it, eh, Danny?' This time his whisper is harsh, eyes glinting under thick brows: *I'm insulting your mother. What you gonna do about it, Danny-Boy? Anything?*

'Gagging for it,' he hisses again because I haven't answered. I'm thinking of my Old Dear sitting beside me wringing her hands, knowing Jakey's suggestion is ludicrous and mean.

'You're sick, Jakey,' I say, trying to force a laugh, although it's me that feels sick at my own spinelessness. Jakey would have pushed the matter further if Sean and Waz, still vying for position before the square of frosted glass on Gubby's door, hadn't fallen against it with a clatter and swung the door ajar.

Gubby's chair scrapes back quickly inside the room, but before he appears in the corridor Jakey has his arm clamped around my shoulder and I'm outside in the yard.

'We're heading for Waz's place.'

I did try to protest. I'm sure I did.

'I can't. My Old Dear's in there.'

Should have seen Jakey's answer coming, shouldn't I?

'Then you've an even bigger reason to scoot than we have, Danny-Boy.'

* * *

It's always the same old routine at Waz's place: making prank calls, messing about in chat rooms. Doesn't matter who you phone on Waz's line. His folks are always away on business, and never check their bills.

Jakey decides who we're going to prank then makes me do the talking because I'm good at voices. Today I call the Academy, pretending I'm a crabby old gerry, complaining about two blond girls (these are the Taylor Twins of fifth year, bursting with brains and beauty) who spat at him at a bus stop. While I'm speaking to the school secretary, Waz, who's always a total bottom feeder in his own house, yells my name down the mouthpiece: 'Henn-e-ssy!'

Jakey's doubled over, laughing. 'The look on your coupon, Danny-Boy,' he says, busy punching in Waz's Old Boy's credit card number to log on to some porn.

Porn makes Waz and Sean catatonic, must be all that blood they need to maintain brainstem function rushing away from their heads. It's as much as they can do to watch the screen and remember to breathe. They don't flinch when the phone rings. And rings.

'Get that, Danny-Boy,' grunts Jakey. 'Mind 'n' say it's a wrong number.'

117

But it's Gubby. Looking for Waz's folks. And I've said 'Hello?' in my own voice.

'Danny?'

The disappointment in Gubby's voice makes me flinch.

'That was the school,' I say to the back of three heads gawping at a tangle of squirming naked flesh.

I think of life-drawing, not started yet. Of my Old Dear's hands twisting, more alarming than the writhing shapes on the monitor. I recall Jakey's suggestions about my Old Dear and Gubby, the way he grinned at me while he waited for my reaction.

Without bothering to explain, I slip out of Waz's house and head back to school.

I'd tell myself this fear I had when I was first taken prisoner would have to shrink once I knew the score with the Japs. You canny feel like that all the time, *I'd tell myself.* You'll go off your head.

Truth is, Richard, as time went on, I got more scared. Not less.

You were always close to death. It was everywhere. Men laying track beside you all day, pegged out the next from sickness, exhaustion. Failing to survive on a handful of rice and a cup of weak tea. And you never did know the score with the Japs. They liked to keep it that way. You were always hearing things you couldnae see. Thumps. Cries. Metal on flesh. Water running. Screams way out in the forest. Blokes who marched beside you today, telling you what they did back home, their lassie's name, how many bairns they had, would be gone tomorrow, never seen again. I kept thinking I'll be next. If sickness doesnae get me, torture will . . .

It's hard inside the old head, living like that, month

after month. Starved. Sick. Covered in sores. Full of parasites. Part of you wants to lie down and die. You even feel envy when some poor soul in your hut forgets to wake up one morning. You're thinking, It's over for him, lucky bastard. And then your mind's working: If we don't tell the guards he's dead yet, we can share out his rice ration between us today.

D'you believe a man can be so hungry, so desperate to survive, that he thinks like that?

15
LIFE-DRAWING

I'm late enough to earn a detention from any other teacher but Miss West. She silences my excuses with a raised hand and a smile. Then she nods me to an easel and leaves me to catch up while she bends over someone else's work, discussing it in a whisper.

Nobody speaks loud in Miss West's class, except Jakey, though he hardly ever turns up. It's not that there's a rule about noise in art. In Mr Pierce's room next door, there's always a riot going on, Piercey's voice booming over the top of it all, making things a million times worse. His racket renders the quiet in Miss West's room physical, like a cloak you put on when you enter her domain. Miss West only ever speaks to the whole class at the beginning of the period, perched up high on her window ledge against the backdrop of jaggy rooftops that I've studied and painted and sketched and moulded a hundred times. Legs swinging against the radiator, her

121

clogs hanging loose from her feet, Miss West explains what she wants us to do while we gather round her in a tight semi-circle. Once we're at work, she spends the rest of the lesson teaching everyone individually.

Life-drawing, eh? So much for a Pamela Anderson lookie-likey. The Academy's rustled up an old man, skin and bone. Eyes closed, he's stretched across three chairs in the middle of the room, head propped up on his hand, a sheet round his dangly bits. He looks more dead than alive, the draped cloth across his hips recalling images of Jesus being taken down from the cross in classical paintings we've studied with Miss West. I can number all his ribs and there's a black, flat-iron-shaped shadow in the hollow where his stomach should be. I'm uncomfortable at first, staring at someone so emaciated. The build of the model reminds me of my Grampa Dan, and not only in his last few months when I could wrap my two hands round his upper arm to shoogle him up the bed.

In my mind's eye I stage my subject beneath an orange sun, and my hand starts to move across the page.

I feather in the head, shading cheekbones and the scoop of eye sockets; spaces where flesh dips and darkens against bone. I sketch the neck, lumpen Adam's apple, drawing out the collarbone to the margins of each knobbly shoulder. He's all sinew, this old guy, no muscle to round in fat with the flat of my charcoal, like when we drew our calves last week. Nothing extends beyond the skeleton.

I'm thinking all this while I work. Wouldn't even be surprised if my lips were moving. Wouldn't care, either. I'm lost, like I'm always lost when I draw as if I'm submerged underwater. All I hear, all that matters are the ideas in my head. Everything beyond that – my folks, school, Jakey – completely, *completely* disappears.

My mind is taking this sketch somewhere else, changing it. I'm seeing, not *this* old man, our life model, but my Grampa Dan, plucked bare and white. The face I draw is not the face I see. The face I draw is one I've seen a million times.

'Now, that's really fine work, Danny. I love your use of shade. Never get that right myself. Can you try and define the whole shape before you draw the features?'

You never hear Miss West arrive. Just a cloud of scent preceding her and she's crouched beside you, tracing the air above your work with her finger, like she wouldn't dare smutch what you've created with her touch.

'You see the life model as thin as that?'

We both jump as the period bell shatters the cloister-like industry of the art room. Next door it sounds like every chair in Piercey's room whummels over at once.

In Miss West's room no one seems distracted by the bell; *we've* still another period to go. The only person to stop working is our model.

'Five minutes,' he says, breaking his pose creakily, and standing up to stretch. He's not a bit like Grampa Dan now. Much taller, broader-shouldered when I see him upright, towering over Miss West while she brings him coffee. He doesn't sound like Grampa Dan, either, our model. He's English, bools-in-the-mooth posh, with one of those deep fruity Mr Kipling voices you hear on telly debates. Funny with it.

'My word, you've given me a *splendid* six-pack!' he kids Wee Blushy Morris who turns so red that all her plukes disappear, her neck sinking into the collar of her shirt like a tortoise with acne.

Flicking his sheet over his shoulder like a sari, he wanders through us all. A posh guru. Dead confident. I mean, you wouldn't catch me chatting to a load of kids who've just drawn me in the scuddy, making jokes about the size of my own nose. When he comes to my easel, he peers in close. I hear him drawing air through his nostrils.

'*Very* Stanley Spencer,' he says, stepping back so swiftly to get a better view that Miss West has to do a wee clog dance to get out of his way. I can tell he's impressed.

'Wouldn't say the face is me,' he says, peering in close again, 'but I *do* like this. Puts me in mind of Japanese prisoners of war.'

I get a clap on the back from Posh Guru for my efforts, and between you and me, I'm well chuffed. Can't remember the last time I got a clap on the back from anyone. In my elation I wonder if I should tell Posh Guru that my Grampa *was* a prisoner of war. That he liked drawing, too. That it's really Grampa I'm seeing while I work today . . . But by the time I decide that for once – since Jakey's not here to sneer at my initiative – I *will* speak up, Posh Guru's moved on.

Break over, he reassumes his pose, morphing into exactly the same position as before. Now I'm the one who's impressed. I get back to work myself, Grampa Dan's image overlaying my vision like a filter.

I could bathe forever in this mood, my senses drifting yet alert, producing shapes I don't remember my brain instructing my fingers to create. It's like the hand that draws is not my hand. My ability is outside and beyond myself.

I'm so engrossed, I'm unaware of Gubby till he bellows my name across the room, 'Out, Hennessy!' much too loud for the rest of the set, who tut. Miss West clasps her hands to her chest. Posh Guru doesn't open his eyes.

Double-stepping to match Gubby's stride as he leads me to the Love Doc, I wish I'd taken my drawing with me while I had the chance.

16
RECORD BREAKERS

A week's passed since the Love Doc formally read me the Riot Act, suspending me for 'absenting myself from school premises without due permission'. Basically she ran me out the school, parting shots pinging at my heels: 'One more strike, Daniel, and you're out.'

Gubby said my Old Dear had suffered enough distress for one day to deal with this carry-on, and phoned my Old Boy to collect me.

He took me for a McDonald's which was more punishment for him than it was for me. He didn't eat. Watched me through narrowed eyes, blowing smoke over my burger. 'You better shape up, Danny. "Don't want to end up on the scrap heap when you've so many chances to make something of your life", as your Grampa used to say to me,' was the extent of the carpeting he delivered. I got the impression he had other things on his mind. Places to go. People to meet. I was holding him up.

This weather, my Old Boy spends hardly any of his free time in the house, which is more than I can say for Jakey. With Waz and Sean both grounded during the suspension we were all given, Jakey's appeared every day this week at different times so I can't plan to be out, one morning hiding in the garden until my Old Boy left for work. The stone Jakey pelted at my window cracked a pane and he called me a tube for taking so long to let him in.

Always after money, he started sifting through the Old Dear's jewellery box yesterday.

'Any of this junk we can sell? Your old nag won't be back for it.'

When I said he couldn't do that, he grabbed a pile of albums from my Old Boy's stack.

'We'll punt some of these, then. There's thousands. All shite. Who's gonna notice?'

That's how I ended up cashing in the savings account Grampa Dan opened for me when I turned thirteen. All thirty-seven quid of it transferred to the Jakey Building Society.

Today he's back for more cash and as I've said before, you can't stop Jakey when he wants to do something. You just have to try and divert him.

I blast 'Eugenic', Jakey's favourite Skarrs track, through the house:

> I'm male
> I'm white
> I'm strong
> I'm pure
> No taint of colour in my genes

and do a quick rummage through all my Old Boy's pockets, scraping together about a tenner in change. Neither action satisfies Jakey. He empties the contents of Grampa Dan's chest of drawers on to the mattress.

'This stuff's crap.'

Old specs fly out of their cases, hitting my drawings on the wall over Jakey's shoulder. He tears open letters, scrunching them into balls when he's read them. Most of Grampa's stuff's official: pension notifications and polling cards amid ancient bankbooks, decades ago red-stamped Account Closed. There are letters from me in there too, written in giant baby characters:

> Dear Grampa,
>
> I hope you are not too sad about granny. Do you like her picture in the red coat I drowd for you
>
> Love and kisses
> Danny

Grampa Dan's written *Danny, age 5* in a corner of my letter in the lightest of pencil strokes as if he didn't want to spoil my handiwork. I can recall him doing it, bent over the kitchen table of his old house, dressed in a white shirt and baggy trousers held up with braces. I was fingering a black tie he'd taken off. It was made of material that gave me a shivery feeling down my spine, and touching it spoilt the sensation of Grampa Dan's fingers tickling the back of my neck.

'*"Love and kisses Danny."* Gay boy.'

My letter's on the floor, under Jakey's foot. Now he's

tipping out an envelope full of photographs and cards.

'She's a dug there, your maw,' says Jakey, stabbing his finger into a photograph of my Old Dear, pregnant, sitting on my Old Boy's knee. They're laughing, his hands over hers on her belly. I'd been thinking the opposite of Jakey myself; how happy my Old Dear seemed. Young. Pretty. Old Boy a bit like me around the eyes. Grampa Dan's there too. He's standing up straight, arm round a wee plump woman I know from photos was my Gran Rosie.

'Disgustin', that,' says Jakey, spearing a hole with his finger though my Old Dear's stomach. Quickly, he rifles through all the other papers in the envelope, cursing their worthlessness: pop-up Christmas cards I made in school, postcards I sent from London that time I went away with Richard in P7 and was so homesick I didn't eat.

'I miss you too, honey,' my Old Dear would start greeting down the phone to me every night until my Old Boy had to cut us off and stop her speaking to me. In the background I could hear Grampa BANGBANGBANGing down. 'Is that Danny? Tell him hallo, will you?'

'Crap,' Jakey says, voice ugly as he sweeps everything

from the bed to the floor. 'Gotta get in here instead.'

It was only a matter of time before he went back to Grampa's locked bedside cabinet. If I were him, I would too. But I wouldn't rock it like that, so the legs shoogled. Or tug the brass handle so hard that it snapped.

'Shit,' says Jakey. The knife he whips out of his sock is one I haven't seen before.

'Nut gave me loan of it. It's for hunting. Beautiful, eh?'

The knife's in a leather sheath, and it's got a curved blade. Horrible-looking thing, way too thick to slide into the lock of the cabinet door, but Jakey chisels at it anyway, ramming with both hands so skelfs of wood shear away and flick up in the air.

'Wait a minute, Jakey.'

I have to intervene. Dry-mouth sick, there's a pathetic warble in my voice. 'Won't be anything in there worth selling. Honest, Jakey.'

Jakey doesn't even acknowledge me. He's thumping behind the cabinet with the handle of the knife, trying to force the thinner back-panel in on itself.

'Leave it, gonna, Jakey?' I dare to raise my voice.

'*Leave it*,' Jakey mimics, kicking the back-panel now. I hear wood cracking.

'Stop it. Don't wreck my Grampa's things.'

Suddenly I'm desperate, *desperate* to get Jakey out of this room. Out of this house once and for all. I'd do anything.

'Look, I'll pick out a few of my Old Boy's albums. Rare ones. We'll sell them.'

Aiming one final kick at the front of Grampa's cabinet, Jakey shoves past me and runs downstairs, scoring the wall with the tip of his knife. 'Move it then, Danny-Boy.'

It's sad, I know, but my Old Boy has his own album cataloguing system. Beside the telly there's this special wee box file my Old Dear gave my Old Boy for their first wedding anniversary with an individual card inside for every album he's bought, giving the tic tac on where and when he found it, and how much he paid for it. The file opens with the rare *signed* Elvis 78, purchased in 1960 at St Peter's Christmas fair for 2d ('Worth hundreds now, Danny'), through to details of the unplayed reissue of Nick Drake's boxed set my Old Boy asked me for last Christmas. ('Just to have, Danny, in case my original records wear out.')

If Jakey gave me five minutes I'd have picked out half a dozen albums that would make a few quid – more than a few quid – no bother. There was something signed by George Harrison, a deleted single by the Sex Pistols that my Old Boy would never let me hear, and a stack of albums – all signed because my Old Boy was a stage door anorak when he was my age. The cream of the collection's a bunch of rare coloured vinyls – punk stuff, still in cellophane. Pristine. Unplayed.

As I say, five minutes and I'd have picked out any of these plums with my eyes shut and it'd likely be years before my Old Boy'd notice since he only plays tapes of the rare stuff. But Jakey doesn't give me the chance. He's already flinging armfuls of records from my Old Boy's shelves into a heap in the centre of the room, chucking albums over his head. I try to shield the pile with my body, because each time Jakey steps backwards his heel cracks another record. These are the really valuable ones; tatty because my Old Boy loves to play them: Gram Parsons, the Undertones, Carol King, the Ramones . . .

'Stop!' An angry reflex forces me to shout Jakey to a halt.

The punk vinyls have just been frisbeed into the back of my neck.

'Quit, Jakey. Let *me* pick some things out.'

You should see the smile I get for standing up to him. Full-on ice and so vicious that I have to look away. I gulp, muttering about how my Old Boy'll go ape if he sees the state of his collection. What I'm really thinking is, my Old Boy never goes ape. And this'll break his heart. No wonder I could hurl.

Look at me.

Look at who I'm with.

Look what I'm letting him get away with.

While I sift out albums to sell I'm thinking: me and Jakey, our friendship's well past its sell-by date. The implications of that make me feel even sicker.

If you could have seen the disgust on Lawrence Hope's face that morning after Taff died. Blokes were swarming round Taff's mat, and him still lying there. Like vultures they poked through Taff's kit snaffling anything useful: a spoon, a rag that might cover your head from the sun, Taff's Bible. That's what you did: picked over a dead man's kit. Tried on his boots for size.

Did it myself if it was a bloke I didnae know.

Survival, you'd call it.

Sickening, Lawrence Hope said. Couldnae stand what we'd become. He was a late conscript like myself. Met him at basic training in Aldershot. Lawrence was from Leeds, a bank clerk in civvy street. Thin, soft-spoken. Never looked the part in uniform.

'HOPELESS,' our first drill-sergeant bawled every time Lawrence tried to pick up his rifle, never mind load it, and the name stuck. Lawrence said he owed that sergeant a pint. A nickname like that was better than armour, he said. No one expected anyone labelled

Hopeless to be brave or intrepid, so he was passed over when any tricky jobs cropped up. If we hadnae been captured, Hopeless and myself might have had an easy war to ourselves, keeping out the heat, if you ken what I mean. Him with his books, me with my sketches, counting the days till we got home.

Once we were prisoners of war, Hopeless and I barely muddled through, although he managed to keep so much in the background he hardly seemed to exist sometimes. Being inconspicuous, he'd get away with all sorts. The only picture I had of my Rosie was ripped up in front of me because Fat Guard saw it poking through a hole in my shirt, but when the guards saw Hopeless daydreaming over a photo of his son in the middle of parade, they let him be.

17
ROCK BOTTOM

It's pouring, my T-shirt and jeans sticking to me, making me judder with cold. The only dry thing on me is the fiver Jakey chucked in my face outside the junk shop. My cut. Ten per cent.

'Fifty quid?' He'd spat the words at me. 'Thought Daddy's records were worth more than that.'

Too right. Worth a lot more.

'Where d'you say you found these, man?' Huck, my Old Boy's mate who owns Vibes, asked Jakey, frowning through his hippy plaits like he recognised me.

'Skip,' Jakey mumbled.

'Sure about that?'

'D'you wanna sale or not?'

'This Elvis record? Where'd that come from?'

'Forgot. Give us twenty quid for it.'

When Huck said we'd need to leave the records with him while he had a better look at them, Jakey pulled down a stand of CDs on his way out. The dame in Jenny's Junk Shop didn't ask any questions. George Harrison's autograph was enough for her. 'Fifty quid the lot, take it or leave it.'

Junk Shop Jenny was bigger than Jakey, crushing notes into his hand while she showed him the door. Even he wasn't going to argue.

Don't ask me why I stick with Jakey when we leave the junk shop and he's got his money, but I do: easier than begging to be excused, perhaps?

'You and me, Danny-Boy, we're gonna do some serious noising-up here,' Jakey announces, hulking towards St Anne's school – where Richard and Ali go – ridiculous looking with my jacket over his head as a rain-mate. Not that I'd say that to his face.

'Check they mingers, Danny-Boy,' he says more than loud enough to panic a group of very small girls into the path of oncoming traffic.

'What you looking at, pizza face?' he yells, blocking this poor geek of a lad, who lollops away on Bambi legs. 'Want me to bend your spine till you're looking up your arse backwards?'

Keep walking, everyone, I'm thinking telepathically.

My own head's well down trailing Jakey, then overtaking him, all nonchalant, every time he stops to insult someone. *Honest, I'm not with him, pal.* That's why I bump into Richard coming out his school gates.

'Hey, Danny, what brings you here? Day off school?'

Another thing I haven't mentioned about Richard is, if he's happy about something, he can't hide it. *Nae side to him*, as Grampa Dan used to say. He's beaming me his big beacon smile today. Typical Richard again: doesn't bear a grudge.

'How you doing anyway, Danny? I was coming to see you today about –'

'Dicky-Head.'

Jakey steps between us, his breadth blocking my view of Richard. 'Not askin' how ah'm doing an' all, Dicky-Head?'

While Jakey speaks he flats both hands against Richard's chest and shoves him backwards. Once, twice, three times, until Richard is forced up against his school railings.

'Where's your manners, Dicky-Head? Talk to me, too, eh? Tell me why you're coming to see Danny-Boy.'

Richard's taken plenty abuse from Jakey in the past:

140

prank phone calls, dog-shit jiffy packs, miscellaneous nastiness, but this is the first time he's been physically threatened. And it happens fast. Over before I know what's what.

Jakey pinning Richard to the railings with one hand.

Hissing into Richard's ear, 'Leave Danny alone, Dicky-Head. He's my mate now.'

Jakey's free hand drawing that big curved hunting knife from a pocket in his trackie trousers.

Richard's hands flying up.

Grabbing Jakey's wrists.

Forcing Jakey's arms against his sides, with a blink-and-you'd-miss-it twist thrown in for good measure.

Jakey's knife clattering to the ground. 'Awww.'

The speed and strength of Richard's reaction jerks Jakey into a curl of pain. While his head's down, Richard brings his knee into swift contact with Jakey's goolies.

'Oo-ya!'

Jakey coils instinctively; a fossil in a shell suit, mouth open in a silent scream of pain. Richard slips past him and saunters away.

'See you later, Danny,' he waves. He's whistling.

Christ, I'm thinking, looking from Jakey to Richard,

141

dead man walking, although there's a wee fella inside me jumping up and down, punching the air in triumph at what Richard's just done. *Gotcha!*

Jakey remains slumped against the railings. 'Look what Dicky-Head's done to my baws,' he moans, tenderly gazing inside the waistband of his trackie bottoms. 'Bloody burst ma tackle. Tell you, Danny-Boy –' the pain in Jakey's voice adds a diamond edge to his threat, 'he's totally dead. Go and get him back now.'

Tricky situation, eh?

If I do what Jakey wants – drag Richard back to get knifed – I think that *might* be straining the limits of our old friendship. On the other hand, if I refuse to do what Jakey asks, then I might as well add my name to the top of Jakey's Most Wanted list. Bracket it with Richard's. Bit of a dilemma.

Luckily I'm saved by the smell.

'Psss. Want any shtuff the day?'

I never thought I could be glad to see Ming Mulholland sidling the railings towards me and Jakey. Normally I give him a major body-swerve, not only because he stinks worse than all the noisome pongs you can think of put together: bad fish, puke on a hot day, dog breath . . . but because he's the local drug dealer.

OK. I'm talking small-time desperado, with a habit of his own to feed. Way down the food chain, a million miles removed from the Hollywood stereotype of a scary bloke in shades driving a long car with blacked-out windows and carrying a piece. Nevertheless Jakey refers to Ming as 'My man', which I find tragic. Ming's the most shilpit specimen of humanity – let alone masculinity – I've ever met; more like a dirty lollipop stick covered in ooze. Normally you smell Ming before you see him, and suddenly he's either huddling beside you offering God knows what in filthy twists of paper, or worse, pulling out pills from the nether regions of his trouser pockets.

Not being into drugs, I've never bought from Ming for my own consumption, but nine times out of ten my money's been used in any transaction going down when I'm with Jakey. That makes me party, doesn't it?

'Good shtuff de day, lads. Meckshican.' Ming talks like there's an invisible clothes-peg on his nose – lucky him – and there's always a phlegmy tremor in his throat that makes me want to arch back even further from him than I do. Trouble is, the further you move from Ming, the closer he moves in, invading your body space.

'Yoush willnae shcore better 'n' 'ish. Make yoush pure float.'

Ming's eyes are always glazed, moving slowly, like a pair of fish in a cloudy bowl as one word slurs into the next. His eyes are at odds with his body, which jerks non-stop, all his nerve-endings on red alert. I feel tired watching him jiggle impatiently over Jakey, who's examining a cluster of pills dancing like jumping beans in Ming's cupped hands.

'Much?' asks Jakey, easing himself from the railings with a groan.

'Fifteen each. I'll gie you shix. She you shrough de weekend.' I've noticed Ming's teeth always chatter when he talks money. Maybe he's scared he won't deal, and then he won't get his cut from whoever pulls his strings. Then he'll miss his next hit. It's pathetic.

'Fifteen? No chance.'

I've never heard Jakey speak like this to Ming before. Usually, given that Ming is the source of what Jakey wants, there's a bit of patter before a deal is struck. But not today. Jakey's venting his anger at Richard on Ming, who's gibbering now, sweat beads spotting his waxy forehead.

'Awright, Jakey, man, but I'm gien' the shtuff away here. Fifty the lot. Canny dae better than 'at or I'm deid. Know what I'm shaying?'

Jakey's hesitation's making Ming nervous. He's still hunched over Jakey with the pills in his hand, but his head's swivelling from side to side like a lizard. He couldn't make the illegality of his behaviour any more obvious if he wore an illuminated sign: Dealer At Work.

'Fifty. Hmmm.'

Jakey strokes his chin. 'For that price we try before we buy. Give Danny here a free sample, an' I'll take the rest for fifty.'

Snap.

Ming's fist closes on the pills in his hand, camouflaging my gulp of consternation.

'Go on, Ming.' Jakey shoves a bunch of notes into the breast pocket of Ming's jacket. It's the money from the sale of my Old Boy's albums.

'Only forty-five here, man.'

Nothing wrong with Ming's mental arithmetic as he counts the money between a filthy thumb and index finger.

'Danny?'

Jakey's nodding at me to hand over the fiver he gave me. The price of my Old Boy's *Sergeant Pepper*, or *Pet Sounds*, *What's Going On*, or *Hunky Dory*. All flogged to the junk shop to buy real junk. I'm at rock bottom now, amn't I?

I mean, what would my Old Dear say if she saw me here? Grampa Dan. What would he think? *Always be your own man, Danny*.

'Fiver, Danny-Boy. Move it.'

Jakey's fingers are snapping so close to my face that the air around my nostrils is displaced. Ming's hand is flat out under my chin as if he's offering a sugar lump to a donkey. There's a blue capsule vibrating there. I can smell Ming's fingers.

'I said fiver, Danny-Boy, and take that bloody jelly before you get us all caught.'

When I make a fist and punch the blue capsule out of Ming's hand, I hope I don't hurt him. He's a poor soul. It's Jakey I wish I'd the balls to punch instead, although by the time I've started running home, him calling after, 'See you later, Danny-Boy,' all my anger's gone and I'm crapping myself.

Hopeless wasnae one bit hopeless, Richard. He was a godsend. Because he was quiet and handless, the Japs didnae reckon him capable of any hanky-panky. So he got himself assigned to mess duties and found all sorts of ways to whip rations from the guards. The risks he took; they'd have had him disembowelled. Buying fruit from the locals outside camp if any of us had money or possessions to trade, stealing meat scraps off the guardroom plates, lifting fishheads from the midden to cook in with our rice.

He'd hide food all over himself: down his shorts, his boots, in his fists. Never well concealed, but the guards took no notice of him.

Bloody daring all the same.

I can see Hopeless now, right in front of me, unfurling these long fingers of his one by one. Smiling. He'd yon quiet smile, a modesty about him, never thinking he'd done anything special: 'Look, Henny. An egg today.'

I'm talking tiny piss-poor amounts of food you could put in your eye by the time Hopeless' stolen grub was shared out, but I swear, it kept me going on that railway. Just getting that wee dod extra… I never collapsed on my shovel like other poor bastards I saw flogged till they got up again. I was weak, but never really sick as plenty round me, shitting their insides out. I survived the labour; mindless, backbreaking work. Clearing forest, dragging logs, hauling sleepers, shifting tons of earth … No pride in my effort, mind. That was the tricky bit. You were making as cackfisted a job as you could, looking as if you were knocking your pan out doing it. Not easy when a gun's poking your neck and a guard's screaming, 'DIG.'

Hopeless showed me the knack of hacking the same patch of earth all day without managing to dig down. Other fellas could lay track that'd spring as soon as a beetle never mind a train ran over it. Hopeless liked to sink termite nests underneath the wooden posts he hammered. My *labour of love*, he called his sabotage.

So, not that hopeless was Lawrence Hope. He was

dished up snippets of news when he dolloped out the rice rations. Details about the hundreds of prisoners a week dying from overwork on the railway. Confirmation of diseases spreading through other camps. One day he heard there was cholera further up the line and the Japs had taken sick prisoners out of their huts and shot them before an epidemic started. Now they were going to move the strongest men from our camp to theirs to replace the sick.

That was when Hopeless said he'd rather take his chances with the snakes than die hacking out new railway track for the enemy. 'I'm done digging,' he said. 'Anyone fancy coming with me?'

18
A HAIRCUT WITH GRAMPA DAN

I don't know what to do with myself when I leave Jakey behind. Scared to go home in case he turns up, I walk the streets in the rain, jacketless. Shivering at my drookit reflection in shop windows.

When I pass Vibes, its neon sign burns a guilty brand into the back of my eyes. Slinking past so hippy Huck doesn't see me, I bump into someone taking shelter beneath the red-and-white striped canopy of the barber's.

'Coming in out the wet, Danny?' says Mister Derek. He's all buttoned up in his wee white coat, drinking tea from a Bob the Builder mug.

'You're soaking,' he says, steering me into his shop before I know it.

'Sit,' he says, flicking stray hairs off one of his

150

swivel seats with the same towel he hands me. His nod indicates that I should dry my hair.

'Don't need a haircut. Only a few weeks since I –' I begin, gripping my fiver tight, but my words are lost in the billow of the cape parachuting down my shoulders as I'm birled round to face the mirror.

It's hot in the shop. Steamy. The floor under my trainers slick with condensation. I'm the only customer. From the way my seat is angled I can look beyond my own reflection, beyond Derek, to a row of empty mirrors. In each one I see the back of my head and my face, duplicated to infinity and beyond.

'Rain's keeping my punters away,' sighs Derek, through air damp and heavy with the sharp, medicated scents of shaving balsam and hairspray. His voice sounds miles off.

'Grampa Dan says they used to dig in rain like this. Soaked to the skin for days. Mud everywhere. Terrible for the feet.' Derek's matter-of-fact voice is very close to my ear, the steel of his scissors cold as they grind on the first snatch of hair between his fingers. A shiver runs through me. I didn't ask Derek to do this, yet I feel completely powerless. The heat, the damp, Derek's faraway voice, the sureness of his touch on my head numbs me and I can't muster up the energy to speak. *Look, my hair's still pretty short* . . . Besides, the things he's saying . . .

'Danny, I've just to give you a short back and sides this time, none of that skinhead malarky.' Derek talks to his fingers. 'You've got your Grampa worried sick about you. All this carry-on with school. No good at all. That nyuk you're knocking around with? Get shot of him before you really go off the rails. Take stock, Danny.'

Not once does Mister Derek glance at my face while he's talking. He's too busy working on my hair, adjusting the tilt of my skull with the lightest touch. Behind me, his wee pot belly cushions my head while he checks my sidies are symmetrical.

I say Mister Derek's talking, and yes, in his own voice. Wee bit lispy, wee bit camp. But the words he uses, the turn of phrase – what would Gubby call it? – the idiolect: it's my Grampa Dan's. No wonder I'm gobsmacked to the point of muteness. Somehow my Grampa Dan is speaking through – or speaking *to* – this barber who's hijacked me into a haircut.

And I'm drinking in every word.

'And you're smoking, Danny, when you know it's a mug's game. Grampa was only smoking at your age because he didnae know any better. No one did, back then, but look at the bother he had with his chest. Isnae that a lesson? Grampa doesnae want you getting hooked like he did. Doesnae want you getting hooked on anything. And you know what he's talking about.'

I can't see Mister Derek's face at all now. He's crouched behind me, snipping at single hairs. I can feel his breath on the nape of my neck when he speaks. First to me: 'That's Grampa away now, Danny. Said his piece. Oh, no, he's back.' Then he speaks to . . .

Well . . .

Scissors poised in mid-air, Mister Derek cocks his head to one side. Eyes closed tight, he frowns, as if he's straining to hear something.

'Take your time, now. Slow down,' he whispers, eyes still closed. 'Who, Dan? Richard? I *know* you've mentioned him before. I'll tell Danny again it's important. Are you listening, Danny?'

For the first time since he started cutting my hair, Mister Derek's talking directly to me, as casual as if he's passing on a phone message. 'You've to speak to Richard.

Soon. And you *listen* to what Grampa says. That's you, Danny. You'll be feeling a lot tidier now.'

You'd think Mister Derek, grinning behind me, had spent the last ten minutes telling me where he took his weans on holiday. Not playing the go-between in a supernatural conversation.

He has his hand-mirror up behind my head, moving it to one side of me and then the other: 'Happy with the length?'

What else can I do but nod? *Yeah, great, thanks.* Sit meek as a lamb while Derek clears the stray hairs from my neck with the soft brush.

'Still wet out there.' Mister Derek turns his head towards the street. For a moment, before he removes the nylon cape, his hands lie on my shoulders, leaning, not resting, and fatigue crosses his face like a shadow. There's a slackness in his eyes and jaw when he sighs, 'He's back again. Does the name Paul mean anything to you, Danny?' as though he's being forced to ask the question against his will. Our eyes connect in the mirror, but there's a challenge in Derek's gaze: *Don't ask, Danny. Just answer. I'm tired.*

'Paul,' I shrug beneath his hands. 'That's my Old Boy.'

'Well, Grampa Dan's worried sick about him. Doesn't understand that Derek only links up visitors at his *proper* sessions, your Grampa Dan. Never at the salon.'

Derek's voice is raised in mock-exasperation. Half in fun, wholly in earnest, he scolds the space around me in a weary sing-song voice, using the cape which he's whipped from my neck to flap the air. As if he's shooing someone away.

Of course there's no one; only me, Derek, and our infinite reflections. I do look round and check. No one.

'He's gone, Danny. Character, eh?' Derek sweeps my paltry hair clippings into a shovel. 'Must be desperate to come through to you, going to the bother of finding a medium, and hassling me here at work.'

'A medium?' I've rediscovered my voice, and all sorts of questions are tumbling over themselves to be asked first. 'How can Grampa Dan talk to you? Can you see him? Where is he? Can *I* talk to him?'

As usual, my timing's impeccable.

The shop door opens with a tinkle, letting in a swoosh of rain.

'With you in two ticks, Mr Anderson,' Derek greets his next customer, gesturing him to the chair beside me.

Towel-swiping any hairs off it before Mr Anderson sits down. I take the hint, reluctantly unfurling my hand.

'Only got a fiver,' I say.

'Away you go. It's not a haircut you needed,' says Derek, waving me towards the door. 'Just remember,' he intercepts me before I leave, 'this isn't a wind-up.' Mister Derek's sharp blue eyes look me straight. 'I never do this for fun, and I don't like loved ones coming through when I'm working. Means it's important.' Derek opens his door for me, handing me an umbrella from a box marked 'Lost Property' on the way out.

'Right home now, Danny,' he says.

Now I'm *really* flummoxed. By the aff-its-heid possibility that my Grampa Dan, most definitely deceased, is passing me messages via Derek Scissorhands, my local psychic barber.

I mean, screw the nut. This is Glasgow . . .

Traffic hurtles by, swooshing filthy spray all over my feet as I trudge for home. To say I'm glum is putting it mildly. My new, unnecessary haircut bristles the back of my neck, and my empty stomach feels as if it's being corroded by its own unemployed digestive juices. But these are minor irritations. Nothing compared to the dread prospect of finding Jakey on the doorstep.

I should be grateful for small mercies. There's no sign of a bloke with my jacket buttoned under his chin practising dissection with a hunting knife when I reach my cul-de-sac.

But once my front door's safely snibbed behind me, I'm more wretched than ever. I mean, how would you feel if you were standing in my squelchy trainers scanning the tangled chaos that used to be the meticulously catalogued soundtrack to my Old Boy's life? Knowing everything was all your fault.

You might feel more miserable than miserable. Is there a word for it? I can't find it anyway, because I'm only just managing to stop myself from having a freak-out at the state of my bombsite living room, when the front door goes.

I freeze, suspended in a spasm of fear.

It's pathetic. *I'm* pathetic, ashamed of the sight of myself in the hall mirror, eyes rounder and wider than my cartoon O of a mouth. *Go away. Please go away*, I beg silently, as the door rattles again.

'Danny, you all right? Shit! What's going on here?'

Things must look even worse than I thought. All the years I've known Richard, I've never heard him swear.

'Shit, Danny,' he says again. When I lift up my hand to see why he's pointing at it, it shakes so much that the blood seeping through my clenched fist drips on to the carpet. Richard opens my fingers, prising a shard of broken vinyl from my grip. I can't even recall picking it off the floor, let alone feeling its edges bite into me when the door knocked.

'Shit, Danny.'

Richard's beginning to sound like a broken record himself. I'm tempted to kid him on – *We'll mind the language in this house if you don't mind, son* – which is what his Old Dear used to say if I let slip a naughty over nursery tea. But when I see the look on his face, I realise there's nothing funny in this situation.

'What's happened?' says Richard, returning the inner sleeve of Kate Bush's *The Kick Inside* to its cover. My Old Boy and I loved that album, listening to it, over and over, me lying on his lap until I fell asleep. Old Dear humming along to the music from the kitchen.

When I reply with no more than a shrug, I can tell by the way Richard sighs that he doesn't need to know any more. 'Danny,' he says, dropping to his knees. If Gubby were to ask me to identify his subtext it would be this: You gotta get shot of Jakey.

Instead he says: 'Let's sort this. Your dad's got enough on his plate.'

Richard and I barely speak during the clear-up. It takes hours, as every record has to be remarried to its cover and lyric sheets, then reshelved. Since my hand is still bleeding, I don't touch anything. Richard told me not to. He sifts the pile in front of me until I spot a match. We used to do the same thing with our Lego: sort a million tiny pieces to build separate creations again: spaceships, submarines, fire stations. It could take us a whole day, or a weekend, but it was always worth it.

Tonight Richard doesn't even ask me how I cut my hand.

When the room is tidy, he leaves, taking any smashed records away with him.

'I'll try to get replacements at the weekend,' he says, seeing himself out.

'Nah, I can do that tomorrow,' I tell him, too busy, calculating how far my fiver will stretch, to check my big mouth.

'You've got school . . .' begins Richard. Then he twigs: 'For God's sake, Danny.'

You gotta sort yourself out, pal. That's his subtext this time. And after the day I've had, I don't like the way his pity makes me feel.

I throw an ungrateful 'Thanks!' at Richard's retreating back, which he dismisses with a weary swipe of his arm. It's only then that it dawns on me to ask him, 'Why d'you come over tonight, anyway?'

Without turning round, Richard fishes in his pocket, pulling out a minidisc, which he waggles at me.

'Was gonna let you hear this,' he says, walking away with his head down, 'but you're not ready yet.'

All this talk of Hopeless escaping; I thought he must have changed his mind because when we were marched further up jungle, he was there at my side. I was that hungry, frazzled by the sun beating down, that it was all I could do to put one foot in front of the other, never mind ask Hopeless what he was up to.

You got that way. One step from breaking point. Done in.

That march to the next camp was hell. A forest walk in the sun, Hopeless called it, and I could barely stand up. Twenty-two years old and I'm thinking, I'm walking to my death here. I'd one of those – och, I don't know what you call it – when you seem to look down on yourself from up high. I'm seeing this ragged soul I don't recognise. Wheezing and panting like a clapped-out dug needing to be put down. Covered in sores. Prodded on with a bayonet if he staggers. I see him stepping round Tom Merry because he's tripped and the guards are skelping him across the back for holding up the line. Tom's trying to curl himself into a ball, but it's useless. There's too many of them.

We're all dead, I'm thinking. Me, Tom, all the other lads. And Hopeless, because he didnae escape after all.

But Hopeless wasnae hopeless. He'd slipped away.

Fat Guard didnae even consider Hopeless capable of escape, assumed he'd collapsed. Sent me and poor, bashed-up Tom Merry to collect him with a guard. We found two lads fallen on the path we'd walked. One dead, one barely alive. Neither was Hopeless but I made a grand show of letting the guard think the dead lad was him. What did the guard care?

We left both men where they lay. Tom Merry told the guard the other lad was dead an' all. Kinder to leave him there, the jungle floor his deathbed, than drag him back with us. Tom whispered this while we crouched over this dying lad, who was trying to talk though he didnae have the breath to get a breath, let alone a word.

Tom Merry said we should pray over him. God knows why, I thought. But I did it anyway. Our Father, who art in heaven. Where the hell are you?

I know what you want to know, Richard: Hopeless?

I don't know, is the answer.

Never felt I could follow anyone up after... Never have. What would we be talking about? Why would we want to trade stories?

19
OPERATION ALI P

Sod's law.

Even if I want to, I can't go to school, yet here I am. Up. Dressed. Wide awake. And it's four *a.m.*, for God's sake.

'That you, Danny?' Grampa Dan would be calling if he heard me tiptoeing to the bog in the wee small hours like this. Last couple of years I'd have deliberately rubber-eared him, thinking to myself: No, you old goat, it's a mad axeman coming to slit your Adam's apple.

Only Grampa's not here, is he? Just my Old Boy, and he doesn't hear me. Too busy snoring. So much for me being all freaked about him coming in and catching Richard and myself mopping up Jakey's mess. He didn't show till after two. I heard a woman's voice calling, 'Night, sweetheart.' Then a car door slammed. I lay tense until I heard my Old Boy's footstep on the stairs. The last thing I wanted him to do tonight was kip in the sitting room with his music on. There's no way of knowing what he'll choose to play. One night it was The Faces, 'You Wear It Well', over and over and over. I mean, it's a cracking song, but after twenty plays . . .

Another night, it was *Sergeant Pepper* – the original *Sergeant Pepper*, now property of Junk Shop Jenny. Yup, 'She's Leaving Home' was played more than once. And lots and lots of Nick Drake. Sad guitar. Plangent strings. Old Boy keeps going back to that, and even I can understand why. But how can he explain the bloody Corrs? It was the Old Dear's CD. I gave to her it last Christmas.

'Torture,' the Old Boy had groaned when the Santa paper came off, though he'd stumped me the dosh to buy it. I'm surprised my Old Dear didn't take it when she left.

Old Boy came right into my room tonight. *Where you been?* I could have asked him, but I played the Sleeping Beauty when I sensed him at my pillow. His hand swept my forehead. I smelt beer on his breath.

'A mess, Danny,' he whispered, remarking, per chance, on the state of my boudoir. But I think not.

I couldn't sleep when the Old Boy left me. I lay in the dark and the inside of my head turned into an Imax cinema.

It was a Hennessy Home Movie Special. Comedy shorts first: me doing the twist with my Gran Rosie, one of the only memories I have of her. Grampa Dan hooching and clapping along to the music.

Then there was a tourist information film: *Don't Come to Scotland*.

Me and the folks, huddled in fleeces, trying to keep the sand out of our picnics, the sole occupants of grubby West Coast beaches in high summer.

Followed by the main presentation: a brooding, atmospheric kitchen-sink drama, charged with long silences, dark glances and snapped responses. It starred the Hennessy family at breakfast less than a week after Grampa Dan's funeral.

Nobody's talking, and I'm the only one eating, making sure I slurp my Rice Crispies max vol to draw some of my Old Dear's most toxic looks. She keeps glaring at my Old Boy, wanting *him* for once to be the parent who instructs me to grow up and show some manners. Instead, the Old Boy slinks out and plugs in his guitar. Out of the blue the Old Dear chucks her mug, full of coffee, at the kitchen door. I kid you not. The brown tracks are still there, like tears, as Smokey sings. And then she says, just like in the movies: 'That's it.'

And leaves.

THE END

After the film show I get myself under the shower until there's no hot water left, then plonk myself in front of crap four a.m. telly.

Now I'm on my fifth mug of tea, and it's morning bright outside. When a movement through the window tears me away from Dallas, I clock Ali Patel closing her front door the way you do when you don't want anyone to hear you. Just after six a.m., how dare she look like that? She's wearing one of those wee cropped running vests and black shorty things that she must have spray-painted on. Bloody gorgeous. And I can proclaim that out loud: '*Bloody gorgeous*!' because there isn't a soul to hear me at this ridiculous hour.

If I had magic, elasticated arms that could pass through glass and stretch, d'you know what I'd do? Reach out and run my hands all over the smooth skin of Ali's torso from her ribs to her jewelled belly button. I'd draw her close until her bare stomach was pressed against me and I could see ugly old Danny reflected in her green eyes. Everything would get a bit blurry as I reached for her mouth, bending to kiss her . . .

But before I get any of that I need to catch her. Ten minutes after she's jogged out of my frame, I'm still holding her in my fantasy arms, wondering if she'll let me do a muscle test on her gluteus maximus. Then my voice of reason has to spoil everything:

Get real, Danny. Ali Patel wouldn't piss on you if you were burning. And anyway, she's doing a line with Richard.

That gets me thinking: Richard and Ali. It's not as if they're married, are they?

Richard and Danny? It's not as if it matters if we fall out over the same girl.

Time I stood up to my voice of reason. After all, I deserve a break.

And I like a challenge.

Danny and Ali: why not?

I knew my skateboard would still be in the garage. Old Dear never throws anything away – apart from twenty years of marriage. Boom! Boom! Since I won't apologise, I'm going to use nostalgia to worm my way back into

Ali's good books. Appeal to the child in her. This is Operation Ali P.

I've just about got the hang of staying upright on a manual again when Ali sprints past me, nearly bowling me over in her slipstream. She's got her head tucked down somewhere near her collarbone. Her eyes on her watch.

'Come on. Come on!' She's panting, oblivious to my shoogly presence, otherwise I doubt she'd be spitting quite so fulsomely into her Old Boy's fuchsia before collapsing on the garden path, legs spread wide in the air. She's obviously used to getting the world to herself at this hour.

It's all a bit too unselfconscious, even for a free thinker like myself, and I *nearly* can't watch when Ali goes through this stretching floorshow that makes Christina's dirrrty dance routines look like Keep Fit for Carmelites.

But then I remember why I'm out here: for once I'm taking Grampa Dan's advice. *'Carpe diem* – seize the day, Danny, because you only get one kick of the can.'

I'm sure Grampa didn't mean me to break my neck when I seized the day. I don't mean it either. I only want Ali to glance up nostalgically as I cruise by, cooler than Johnny Knoxville, throwing her a nonchalant wave. *Hey, remember this, Ali? Wanna show me if you can still kickflip?*

Instead, I get one foot on my board and it skites off from under me, taking me down as though I've slipped on a giant banana skin.

'Whoaw.'

My wimpy cry of panic is the last sound I recall as I wheech downhill towards Ali's garden path, stopping only when one of my size twelves pistons into her outstretched groin and my head strikes the base of her Old Boy's mock-Grecian planter.

As I come to, Ali's resuscitating running shoe is kicking lumps out of me.

'What you doing on a skateboard, Hennessy? You were only ever good at drawing them. Not riding them.'

Even when she's insulting me, she's got a brilliant voice, Ali Patel. Gruff, like she's been shouting along to her favourite band all night. I could lie here all day and let her shout at me.

I think I might actually have to lie here all day. Can't feel my legs – though that's only because they've been kicked numb – and I'm woozy. My focus is so blurred that the clouds above my head are contracting and expanding as though they're breathing in and out.

'Now you're bleeding, you prat,' says Ali when I try to sit up.

It might not be love, but at least she cares enough to lean over me. She's got sweat on her collarbone. It shines like lustre. Two salty drops land on my lips. Nectar. I flick out my tongue and lick the droplets away.

Carpe diem.

'Hey, you with me, Hennessy?'

Ali pinches my chin between finger and thumb. Not gently. I can feel her bare thigh pressed against my side.

'Your head's bleeding, Danny.'

I could be imagining – after all, I've just thumped my noddle – but I swear, there's concern in Ali's voice. I check her green eyes, just to make sure, and when Ali Patel stares back . . . Well, there's a glimmer. *Definitely* a glimmer of . . . Well, how the hell would I know? I'm no expert. But it's something. A surge. Electric.

Who would have thought it?

Me and Ali Patel.

Something.

Maybe.

Definitely maybe.

'See, if you need stitches, Hennessy, I'm not taking you to casualty,' Ali says, yanking me to my feet. She shoves my skateboard under my arm. 'Here. Desperate Dan, stick to drawing,' she grins.

Honest, I'm not at it when I stagger. I'm so dizzy, I grab for Ali's shoulder to save me stumbling.

'Hey,' she says, putting her arm round my back until I seem steady.

'Rusty,' I say, raising my skateboard apologetically, when she turns to go inside. *Wait*, my heart's begging her. *Let me see you later.*

'Hey, Ali,' I call after her, 'look, I'm sorry.'

Good man, Hopeless. Be grand to think he made it back to his wee lad. Lawrie was his name. See, today, if you gave me a pencil, I could still draw that wee lad's photo from memory.

I did that a lot for folk. How I got into hot water.

I only started sketching when I was posted overseas. Used to do cartoons of the lads for fags. Kept me going. Killed the boredom, because before they mobilised us to Burma, we did nothing but sit on our arses, waiting for something to happen. I found that tough, always thinking of home. Rosie. We all had our own ways of dealing with being away. Some blokes had their Bibles, others spent their days writing letters to their lassies. Others ran round the parade ground like hamsters on a wheel before the sun fried them. Then they'd snore the rest of the day away under their mosquito nets. Don't get me wrong, Richard; there was drill, square bashing, inspections. All the usual Army palaver, but in India, the war never felt close. Used to rile plenty of the lads: they were here to see action. Sitting around wasnae what they'd trained for.

Me? I was happy to be out of the firing line. I'd think, if all that's going to kill me is boredom, I can live with that. And anyway, I could draw to thole the monotony.

Not that I'd ever drawn more than a dirty look back home before the war, in case you're thinking I was some kind of artist like our Danny could be if he put his mind to it. Schooling for lads like me in the thirties meant you had the three Rs belted into you and out the door at fourteen. I look at Danny – you'll be the same – and he's learning science and French, and when he was still talking to me he'd want me to listen to the speeches he was writing for debates: This House Believes All Nuclear Weapons Should Be Destroyed. Argue *against* me, *Grampa*, he says. And he's bringing me back models of his hand made out of clay, and pictures he's copied from Old Masters. Magic, I think they are, not that I know anything. Still, I've kept them all. See them up the wall there, getting better and better as he gets older. Look, there's his take on yon plain lassie they queue up to see in Paris. Moany Lisa. Danny gave her eyes a right saucy glint, finer than the real thing any day.

This isnae what you're after, Richard, but I tell you, and I'd tell Danny now if only he'd stay long enough for me to get a word out: If I had the start you two are getting, this whole story would be different.

I'd have made something of myself.

Might even have gone into the war as an officer.

But I didnae have the key.

Education.

You've both got it.

Willnae protect you from capture, or torture, or disease. But by God, it ups your odds.

Gives you the chance to make the most of what you've got.

20
WHY DON'T YOU DO RIGHT?

All I've done is apologise to Ali. Kissed and made up, minus the kissing. Nothing to feel guilty about as far as Richard is concerned. I mean, he won't be *serious* about Ali. At fifteen? He's way too focussed on getting to Uni without complications of the heart. And he's never had problems sharing with me before.

He'll be cool.

That's what I tell myself when he calls round after school.

'What's happened to you now, Danny?'

'Nothing. Is my hair all standing up?'

When I check the mirror I see why Richard's eyes are dangling from their sockets on springs. The gash on my forehead's been proving like dough in a warm larder.

'You been in a fight today?' Richard's pop-eyes are all concern.

I could have lied: *Yeah, and you should see the state of the other guy,* but I'm too busy thinking, Ali Patel hasn't told her boyfriend she met me skateboarding. Why not?

'Slipped.' I say, airily, ''S nothing.'

'Aye, right,' says Richard, his I-don't-believe-you purse and disappointed smile jogging memories of similar disappointed smiles I've seen on the Old Dear, on Gubby . . .

'Did Jakey do this, Danny?'

Richard's question reminds me of Jakey's ominous absence these last few days. Won't be a good sign, I admit to myself, aware of Richard's fingers under my chin tilting it up to get a better look at my injury. He's a heck of a lot more gentle than Ali Patel, but his actions remind me of something else; *her* touch while her sweaty thigh pressed against my leg. I remember he's going out with her and I'm not. I jerk my head away.

'Mother Hen.'

'Just want to see if you need . . .'

'Don't need *anything*, Richard. What you here for, anyway?'

'Thought we could sort out your dad's records before the shops shut, Danny.'

Richard sounds hurt, the way he used to when I'd cycle off on his mountain bike after promising it was his turn next. 'Whatever,' I shrug. Jakey would have me pinned to the floor gasping for air if I treated him with such disdain. *What did you say to me, Danny-Boy?*

Richard, however, lets it pass. 'You never know, Danny. The valuable records might still be in the junk shop.'

So we head.

Three of us.

Ali Patel meets us on the way.

'What's happening, Rich?' she asks. Maybe I'm fantasising but I swear she keeps throwing glances at me while she tries to keep her eyes on him.

'Long story,' says Richard, waving his hand airily. 'Danny took the wrong box to the junk shop yesterday. Sold some of his dad's records by mistake. Need to buy them back before Mr Hennessy finds out.' I'm impressed at how plausibly Richard's covered for me when he didn't have to. Even more impressed when he changes the subject altogether. 'Seen the state of Danny's face, Ali?'

'What happened to you?' Ali Patel asks me knowingly. She's fallen into step between me and Richard like Dorothy Lamour in one of those Bob Hope and Bing Crosby adventures I used to watch with Grampa Dan. I keep checking to see if Richard holds her hand. He doesn't, although, curiously yet not unpleasantly, Ali's arm keeps brushing against mine. Too often to be coincidental.

'You're still bleeding,' she says, stopping me while Richard ploughs on ahead. And she touches my temple, much more gently than this morning.

'Danny,' she whispers, her green eyes confused.

Grampa Dan would have called Junk Shop Jenny a big brammer of a wumman. *She* doesn't whisper to me.

'Scram. Oot. Skedaddle,' she bellows, advancing from her back shop. 'Telt your pal no' to come back in here again, now he's the cheek to sends youz in.'

Richard, Ali and I retreat in a backward tangle as Junk Shop Jenny shoos us on to the pavement like vermin at the end of her broom. Every time she flicks out an arm, her oxter expels a mushroom cloud of poison gas in our faces.

Undeterred, Richard wedges his foot into the door.

'Excuse me, miss,' he says in his politest voice. 'My friend sold you those records by mistake yesterday. I'd like to buy them back.' Not only is Richard's foot wedged in the door now, but he's squeezed his hand through the space. And he's brandishing money: a wad of fivers and tenners, *definitely* more than fifty quid. I'd no idea he was going to do this: put up his own money to pay for my stupidity. Nor that he could be so slick with the verbals. I was always the patter merchant in the past.

'My friend's in trouble with his dad for selling you these records. Please sell them back. There's eighty pounds here.'

Unmoved by Richard's grovelling, Jenny slams her door on his money. 'Bugger off, the lot of you,' she growls from the other side of the glass. 'Yon hairy fella next door's beat you to it. Away and pester him.'

'Dumb,' says the hairy fella next door, a.k.a. Huck, from Vibes. He's looking at me.

'Finally,' mutters Ali, checking her watch. We've been at Huck's counter for at least ten minutes waiting for him to open his eyes and stop twitching his head in time to whatever's happening in between his giant earphones.

I'm used to this behaviour. Huck won't serve a customer until he's heard enough of whatever he's listening to. He's all yours, however, when he looks into your eyes and delivers a one-word verdict on the music in his head.

'Salty.'

'Nippy.'

'Minty.'

'Dumb.'

That's why I don't think Huck's comment while we're all waiting has anything to do with me at first, but when he repeats himself – which he never does – 'Dumb. Dumb. Dumb,' I get a bit twitchy myself.

'It's your dad's life, man,' he says. Now there's no dubiety. He's talking to me.

Huck's the tallest guy I know, although his height is disproportionately exaggerated by being the only thing in his shop not stored in an album-sized pigeon-hole. Still, it's scary having him lean over me, the bobbles at the end of his plaits flicking my nose reprovingly as he shakes his head.

'How could you do that to him? Man. 'S like stampin'' on him again, when he's already down.'

That's all Huck's prepared to say for the moment. He turns his back and sets his shoulders against me, busy returning an album to its sleeve. I notice it's one of the Old Boy's all-time favourites: *Astral Weeks*, by Van Morrison. My Old Dear hates it.

'Crap,' she calls it.

'Celestial,' Huck mumbles, stroking the cover before filing it in a space on a high shelf that he negotiates by touch. He draws down a different album, another of my Old Boy's Desert Island Discs: *Blue* by Joni Mitchell, our copy no longer in one piece.

You're doing this deliberately, I mutter, not that Huck can hear me. His cans are on, his eyes are shut, his lips are moving silently in synch with the stylus gently bumping over the record on the turntable.

Huck's oblivious to Richard's polite 'Excuse me. We're looking for the records you bought from the junk shop.'

He's numb to Ali's husky plea as she tugs at the sleeve of his denim shirt, 'Hey, gonna help us, please?'

'What now?' asks Richard.

'Maybe he's put the records out on the shelves already,' says Ali. She wanders off among the racks, leaving Richard to stare at Huck expectantly. When Huck's eyes fail to open after five minutes, he drifts after Ali, leaving me alone at the counter.

'Sucks. What you did, man.'

One eye opens, its pupil wide in the gloom of the shop.

'I'm gonna get those records back safe to your dad.'

Slowly Huck's other eye opens, its pupil smaller, orbited by a ring of pale blue, giving Huck a bit of a gentle space-alien stare.

'She charged me two hundred, man.'

I hear myself splutter protest, *'But we only got paid fifty. I don't have that kind of . . .'*

'Earn it then, man, like I do,' he says sleepily in a faraway voice. 'Work here the next five Saturdays.'

Vibes is a labyrinth. Since it's painted black, dimly lit, and always swirling with psychedelic sound, it's easy to feel disorientated once you move away from the counter. I can't find Richard or Ali, although I'm sure I hear Ali's sexy sandpaper voice giggling through a vinyl wall. Between all these dusty lyric sheets, any kind of hanky-panky could be perpetrated, and I'm having none of it.

'You guys?' I call, my tone reminding me of my Old Dear when she's suspicious: *What are you up to in there, Danny?*

I'm so busy listening out for the would-be lovers that I fail to notice this bloke cross-legged on the floor, reading an album cover, until I've tripped over him and gone flying, head first, into a shelf of Hard Rock and Blues, headering its contents into yet another corridor of music. Through the gap I've made with my bonce is a face I know.

'Danny! This explains why your Grampa Dan's coming through, telling me he loves Peggy Lee singing "Why Don't You Do Right?"'

Psychic Derek the Barber beams through the hole in the shelf.

'How's Paul doing the now, Danny?' he asks, but, of course, it's not Derek who's asking. It's Grampa Dan's question that hangs in the air. I don't mean I hear him like in films where a character opens their mouth and somebody else's voice comes out. That's creepy. This isn't.

It's natural and matter-of-fact. Matter of fact, Derek's not even looking at me when he speaks. He's scooping up the records that my fall scattered, as if he's discreetly keeping out of a private conversation. He behaved the same way in the salon the other day, concentrating on my hair while he let Grampa Dan through.

'Grampa wishes he could let Paul know how sad he is about Susan leaving,' Mister Derek sighs. He's got no shoulders, just a mass of rounded flesh, curved from the neck like one of those padded coat-hangers filled with stinky lavender. Yet when he sighs, his shoulders seem to heave up and widen, the way Grampa Dan's, dog tired after a sleepless night, would work to suck back in some quality of life along with fresh air.

'That's some cut on your hcid, Danny. At least she was worth it.'

Derek chortles, privately: Grampa watching reruns of Morecambe and Wise. He's slotting albums into the space between us. Soon I won't be able to see him any more.

'How can you hear my Grampa? Did you cut his hair?' I call through the closing gap, knowing my second question is pointless. My Old Boy used special clippers. Every fourth Sunday.

Ignoring my question, anyway, Derek looks beyond my shoulder at something, his face dimpled in a grin. There wasn't enough spare flesh on Grampa Dan's face for dimples, but it's my Grampa's smile I'm seeing. I turn, and as I do I hear the gap behind me plugged.

'Richard's the key, Danny.' Derek's voice is muffled. He's gone.

'There you are,' says Richard, with a welcoming clap on the shoulder. 'Were you talking to Ali? I've lost her.'

Who was I talking to? I'm shaking my own head in disbelief as I trail after Richard. 'I think Grampa Dan was here,' I mumble.

'What?' says Richard, not paying attention because Ali stumbles backwards into the pair of us, reading the playlist on a gatefold sleeve.

'Look. Got my dad's birthday sorted,' she says, showing us the front cover of the album: *Peggy Lee and Her Boys*. 'Sticking right out of one of the shelves. Where have you two been, anyway?'

21
HOME TRUTHS

Not bad, I'm thinking, when I get back to my place with Richard and Ali. My Old Boy's records safe with Huck and, between my fiver and a loan from Richard, the broken ones replaced. No sign of Jakey either, I realise, with unbelievable relief. No message bleeping a threat on the answering machine: *Oi, Danny-Boy. I'm looking for you.*

Off the hook, Dan-the-man!

And it feels good that the three of us – me, Richard, Ali – are here, like we're five years younger, and have spent the evening perfecting ollies on our skateboards.

'Look, guys,' I tell Richard and Ali, digging out boxes from the freezer. 'Just like old times: fish fingers and oven chips. The Usual.'

Except the chef's new. I catch the glance I'm not meant to see between Ali and Richard, and kid on I don't, footering with the pilot switch for the grill.

Swearing at the belch of gas that sears me.

The Usual. My Old Dear always said it in mock exasperation when Richard and I breenged in for food. She'd bang the tomato ketchup on the table with a sigh. I used to beat her to it, imitate her shaking her head. Plonking down the loaf of white bread without plates. *Suppose you don't want any cutlery either, you lot?* I'd say, rolling my eyes and tutting. That would crack Ali up; she'd never get away with mimicking her folks in front of them.

'Your mum's funny, Danny.'

Waiting for the fish fingers to cook, I try to remember what my Old Dear looks like when she's laughing. Soon as I picture her, my head clogs up with the memory of her huddled in Gubby's office, straggly hair hanging over her face, twisting her fingers around each other.

To clear that image away I need Skarrs. When I play them through the Old Boy's brand-new, post-Old Dear speaker system, Seth's voice fills every room in the house.

> *You're a black witch baby but I can't say no.*
> *I'm your prisoner under a green-eyed spell.*
> *You're no good for me but I can't let go.*

Gonna drag me down with you into HELL.

'What you playing that for, Danny?'

Richard shoulders me aside to get to the CD controls, twiddling all the wrong knobs to find the off switch. He boosts the volume instead and Skarrs floods the house louder than it's ever been played before.

> *Black witch, queen bitch*
> *Not white enough for me*
> *Black witch, queen bitch*
> *Uncast your spell and leave me b–*

The music cuts, leaving the air ringing with silence.

'Danny!' Richard whispers, gesturing at the kitchen. 'How can you listen to that racist crap, especially when Ali . . .?'

'Just a song,' I breeze, but the door closes on my face. On the other side, Richard's talking earnestly to Ali. I've blown it, haven't I? Two backs turned to me when I follow Richard into the kitchen.

'These are cooked, Danny.'

Ali doesn't look at me when she hands me the

fish slice. 'But I'm heading,' she says.

'Won't be long here, Ali.' Richard smiles, the grim look he throws at me implying that he's got something to say before he leaves. Maybe that's why I follow Ali out into the hall.

'Look, it's only music, Ali.'

'Aye, right.'

'I didn't think it . . .'

'Danny, you never *think*.'

Ali's beeling. I know by the way she spits out my name: *Danny*. But at least she said it. Means she knows I exist, although she keeps her back to me, head down. I follow her to my front door, staring at the nape of her neck, at her olive skin bisected by a twisted leather thong. She's too busy twiddling at my door catch with the Peggy Lee album in one hand to know I've reached out to touch the top of her spine.

'Hope your Old Man likes the record, it was one of my Grampa's favourites,' I say, lifting my arms over Ali's shoulders to open the door for her. And here's the good bit. She has to step backwards to let the door open, and – stroke of tactical genius here – I don't move to give her enough space. I should, but I don't. So she ends up pressed against me just long enough for me to smell her hair. I tell you, my legs turn to water, having her so close.

Now maybe I'm wrong, but if there was a sliding scale produced by some Phd spoffo, evaluating how quickly one human recoils from another following undesired contact, I don't reckon Ali Patel would score top marks. I could bet my limited-edition, signed Skarrs poster that she leans infinitesimally against me. I kid you not.

'You're a very bad boy, Danny,' she whispers.

Her observation, surprise, surprise, is the nub of the pep talk Richard delivers when I rejoin him. Me being me, a very bad boy, I'm used to pep talks. I'd get at least one daily dose from my Old Dear, the way some mothers give their kids vitamins. I'm so used to these nippy nag-ins that my brain's programmed to trip automatically.

Click.

Richard's pep talk, initially, is Richard being straight with me. 'Danny, you're way out of line,' he begins – and I'll be frank: to my surprise, his criticism hurts more than an undeserved dead leg from Jakey; almost hurts more than the realisation I'll never chat to Grampa Dan again, or catch the look on his face when 'Stardust' plays. *Even* hurts more than the weird pain that's not a pain which congests my chest when I start thinking about the Old Dear, the Old Boy, school, Jakey, the whole ballsed-up way things are . . .

I won't regurgitate everything Richard says. Basically, it's a variation on the theme I get from anyone who wants to sort me out:

You're a decent bloke gone bad.

You got problems with your mum and dad.

You're hiding what you really feel.

You're running with a bad crowd.

Face the truth:

You need to change.

Before your life goes down the pan.

Get the picture? Or rather, get the tune; kind of 'Lean on Me', sampling the chorus of the *Friends* theme, and a melancholy 'Moby-esque' break.

Performed without a trace of irony.

Heard it all before.

Until Richard steps up a gear.

'Jakey is bad news,' Richard says. 'He's corrupting you. You never used to be cynical, Danny. Slagging everything off. You'd never have thought it was cool to like a sexist, racist band like Skarrs.'

Point of information, I interject at this point. 'Skarrs aren't trash; they're brilliant. At least they have opinions,' I say, 'and they make people sit up and listen. They're controversial, like Elvis was, or the Beatles, or the Stones, or the Clash, or the Sex Pistols, or ska bands in the eighties . . .'

'Bollocks, Danny.' Richard cuts me off. 'Seth Lamprey's got no talent. He shouts a lot. He's tattooed and pierced and his hair's dyed. That's all. It's surface. He attracts impressionable prats who haven't the wit to invent any rebellious ideas of their own. Once he's got their attention, he knows all he has to do is keep spewing out any crap that comes into his head and his fans'll lap it up. He's laughing all the way to the bank.'

'*I'm* not impressionable,' I say weakly. 'Anyway, it's only music. And you wanna hear yourself, Richard, moaning like an old fart,' I sneer. 'You don't even listen to Skarrs. My Old Dear goes on like you, and she knows nothing either –'

'Danny,' Richard leans across the kitchen table, bringing his face too close to mine for my liking, 'I've got the lyrics to every song Skarrs've recorded. Believe me; I *know* they're crap.'

To my surprise Richard's decibel level's creeping up, the Giant Smartie danger spots on his cheeks pulsing.

'I was doing a website search on prisoners of war for my history project. Guess what came up? That Skarrs track about breaking people in a labour camp I've heard you play. You could click on their video to see *your* band stomping in jackboots and smart uniforms shoving prisoners about and beating them. I mean, Danny, have you *seen* archive film of these work camps? Have you any idea? Did you ever try talking to Grampa Dan about what it was really like? Because I did –'

Richard thumps his fist down so hard on my kitchen table that my Coke can leaps on to the floor and erupts.

'I don't know what's going on with you, Danny. You played that stuff in front of Grampa Dan, and now you put on a racist song in front of Ali. She's your friend . . .'

'I'd never think anything like that about Ali . . .' I cut in quickly. Can you blame me? There's only so much righteous indignation I can take. And I'll tell you this, it shuts Richard up for ten seconds.

'I really like Ali, Richard. We get on great.'

It's too, too irresistible. I can't ignore the chance to sow the wormy seed of jealousy in St Richard's mind, changing the subject while I'm at it. Richard deserves it, doesn't he? Look what he's said about me?

Corrupted. Racist. Trouble.

'I'm gonna get Ali back into skateboarding. We were talking about it this morning.'

'This morning?'

Richard's in my face quicker than Jakey when he smells dinner money in a first year's pocket.

'Aye. That's how I bashed my face. Me and Ali had a wee crash. Didn't she say?'

Now I've really gone too far. Even while I'm speaking, my voice sounds strangulated and Richard hasn't laid a finger on me . . . yet.

'Don't you go near her, Danny. If you touch her, I'm not kidding, I'll . . .'

Before Richard morphs completely into a Tarantino heavy, a key scrapes the lock.

'Hi, stranger.' My Old Boy beams at Richard, his warm glow of greeting clearly blurring his eyesight because I'm flat to the kitchen wall with a fist at my throat. Forced to back away, Richard doesn't stop glaring at me till my Old Boy grasps his shoulder in welcome.

'Great to see you,' says the Old Boy, and they're off, a pair of old muckers, Richard wondering if my Old Boy thinks Neil Young influenced Mercury Rev. You wanna see the chuffed look on my Old Boy's face at being consulted on music. He trots Richard into the sitting room as if I'm the invisible man. An hour later, when they're still holed up together and I have a listen-in at the door, I think my ears are playing tricks on me.

'Things are tough,' my Old Boy's telling Richard, over Percy Sledge giving it 'When A Man Loves A Woman'. 'I know Susan and I weren't getting on for years, but I never thought she'd leave. You get used to somebody being around, end up taking them for granted. I wish she'd come back, Richard. Danny needs her. I'm useless to him.'

You know, it was beauty got me sketching, not horror. Here was I, City Bakery van driver, never out of Glasgow, and suddenly I'm halfway across the world. Billeted with all these blokes already sounding foreign to me: Geordies, Northern Irish, Liverpool, Highland…

I'm only over my seasickness and we're docking in India. Sweltering, it was, shirt sticking to me with sweat instead of Scottish rain. And I'm sleeping out of doors, and I'm seeing brown skin for the first time. Hearing places I've never heard of: Madras, Quetta, Chittagong. Bloody hell! Cities I've to look up in the atlas and keep my finger under to pronounce, trying to figure out the scale, then measuring how far away they are from Scotland on the map.

I take trains with open carriages that rock for days through dark valleys I think'll never end, till we pull into stations. Then natives swamp us, jabbering and touching and offering tea and fruits and sherbet. I couldnae take in the foreignness of everything: the sky bluer than home, the rain blattering to a flood when it fell. Birdsong was new, trees were different. You could have telt me we'd sailed to another planet and I'd have believed you. I'm so taken in wi' everything going on that I start to forget I'm a soldier at war. Whenever I remember, this wee ball of fear rolls up my throat and chokes me.

We're switched from trains to rickety trucks, me an army driver now, part of a convoy bumping through jungle roads. There are lakes where we stop and set up camp, stripping to swim, and the water's warm like a Sunday bath. There's streams and waterfalls plunging through the heat of the day, steam rising off them thicker than my mother's broth.

Faraway mountains poke the sky, snow on their peaks: hot enough to fry eggs on your arm, yet there's snow on the mountains! I nearly run my truck off the road looking at them, taking it all in, moving from India towards Burma and the Japs.

Me babbling like this shows you I'm not one for words, Richard. Never was. Not like Sammy Orr, knocking out his poems about the landscape, lips moving as he wrote. 'This is something to remember, eh, Henny?'

Others, like Hopeless, kept diaries. All destroyed. I'd watch them taking in the wonder like myself, then trying to set it down on paper.

22
SINGING TO MY OLD BOY'S TUNE

No wonder the Old Boy's not talking to me. There's a box at the front door. I spot it when Richard leaves. It's square, album-sized. Scrawled over with one of those pens that Jakey nicks from Gubby's desk to sniff:

VIBES

PAUL HENNESSY TO COLLECT
NOT FOR RETAIL

I'm about to learn that even a mellow geezer like my Old Boy has a breaking point. 'Get in here, please, Danny,' he calls when he's waved his cheery-byes to Richard.

Unlike a glass-shattering siren summons from my Old

Dear, the Old Boy calls me quietly. Slouched in a duvet on the settee, his feet, miserable in holey socks, are propped on the coffee table, big acoustic guitar covering his torso like a shield. Across the strings, his right hand picks a tune, as if it's saying *don't involve me in this unpleasantness*. The knuckles of his left hand, however, strain white through the skin, squeezing the neck of his instrument. Funny I notice that. Even funnier is the fact that I'm, for want of a better expression, bricking it.

'You stole from me, son,' my Old Boy's voice rumbles. *Son.* He's never called me that. Makes me feel about three – in years and centimetres. His big toe, peeping through his sock, points to his record collection. 'Why?'

The Old Boy barely looks up. He's concentrating on the fingers of his left hand, playing something beautiful; the opening of Nick Drake's 'Fruit Tree', I think, but embellished, because my Old Boy loves to improvise and the tune he invents is so delicate I almost forget why I'm here in the first place.

'Why, I asked you, son. I want an answer.'

There's a cold bite to my Old Boy's voice so at odds with the other vibe he's producing that it puts the shivers up me. To think I've always assumed those special pupils of his rip the piss.

'Still waiting, son.'

'Wanted money.'

'Money for what?'

The tune has changed to something complex and circular, maybe Bach. My Old Boy lowers his ear to the strings. His eyes are tight shut.

'Money for what? Come on.'

The tune begins again. The Old Boy squints up at me.

'Sweets? Clothes? Tell me what you needed to buy.'

'Stuff.'

'What stuff?'

With one flick my Old Boy rips down the open strings with his fingernails and lays the guitar on the floor. He sits up, then leans forward, threatening in his next movement to haul himself from his dip in the settee. 'Why did you want money so much that you had to steal?'

For the first time, my Old Boy fixes his eyes on me. Before I can help myself, I'm blabbing . . .

'Wasn't my idea. Jakey wanted stuff . . .'

'*Stuff*? What *stuff*? Why would you let Jakey go through my property? You have no right . . .'

If my Old Boy only knew the half of it! In my mind's eye I see Jakey rifling every nook and cranny in the house. Me bleating helplessly: 'Stop, gonna . . .'

Never again, I think. And I know this makes me a grassing dweeb but I have to give the Old Boy something to get him off my back.

'Jakey wanted to buy cider,' I lie.

'You sold my records for *cider*?'

For a split second I'm thick enough to think the Old Boy's bought it, because he sort of laughs to himself as if he might be thinking. *Och, you boys, wee scallywags!*

Alas, he doesn't say anything like that. Instead he drops a bombshell. And here's Jakey always telling me that parents button up the back.

'Take it you were with Jakey when he bought his drugs, son? Don't even bother trying to deny it.'

I could have lied. I've had years of practice. Instead, I hear myself sing like the wimpy bird to my mild-mannered Old Boy: 'Yeah, I was there, but I didn't take anything. Swear.'

I am so dead.

There must be some fancy Latin word for being

slaughtered by your thug of a mate: Jakeycide? Unfortunately I won't be around long enough to consult my Latin dictionary.

To my Old Boy's gentle guitar accompaniment, I've told him everything:

Where Jakey met Ming. *Tra la la.*

How Jakey spent the record money. *Tra la lee.*

Jakey's mother's name. *Tra la la, tra lee.*

Oh! And her phone number. *Bom bom.*

I am so dead.

'Disappear,' my Old Boy growls, thumbing me towards the garden as he picks up the phone. I don't argue, although I watch him through the kitchen window, the beginnings of a beezer headache pulsing over my left brow while he talks to someone for ages. I light the last fag in my packet, the first draw making my temple beat. Tonight, nicotine tastes too bitter for the back of my throat. I drop the fag and grind it out with my heel.

I'm not the only one watching the Old Boy while he talks. He's giving himself the once-over in the hall mirror, redistributing his single-digit hair quota across his sunroof, poking at the bags under his eyes, as if that'll make them go away. Bizarre as it seems, I can't help feeling that his self-scrutiny is the action of a middle-aged man preening to pass muster with a dame.

Surely, this can't be as a result of speaking to Jakey's Old Dear?

I've met her once. Sunbed skin. Big voice. Bigger hair. She could be Lily Savage's twin . . .

'Locked out, Hennessy?'

Jeez. Fright boosts my headache so it nearly bursts through my cranium when a voice speaks behind me. It's not Jakey, but try telling my nerves that. I hope Ali Patel can't hear my teeth chattering.

She rolls her skateboard trucks across the front of my shoulders. 'Remember how to grind, Danny?'

Grind? I can barely see my hand in front of my face, but I'm hardly skittering back inside whimpering, 'It's too dark,' when Ali Patel wants me to come out and play. *Carpe diem, carpe night-em*, headache and imminent death-by-Jakey or not, I can't pass up the chance to use the cloak of darkness and crash into Ali Patel as many times as I can get away with.

Following her across the street to her place, I

observe how dark her house looks inside.

'Mum and Dad went out,' she says, riding a graceful circle around me, her fingertips dappling the nape of my neck. Making me shiver in a way I've never shivered before.

'So is Richard coming over too?' The stouning of my heart and my head is almost too much. I hold my breath for Ali's reply.

'He's studying,' she sighs, with the merest hint of exasperation.

'What a guy,' I exhale, bitch that I am. 'Doesn't know what he's missing.'

Not that I have much fun outside. My headache goes from bad to worse, thanks to the battery of security lights around Ali's garden clicking on like zillion-watt showgirls everywhere I turn. I have to keep flinging my arms up to protect my eyes, losing my balance.

'Giving up, Hennessy?'

Blessedly, as I crawl on to a step I haven't once grinded, the garden clicks into darkness. Ali drops her deck, waving her arm to reactivate the torturing light show.

'Wait,' I say, reaching out to her.

You won't believe this. *I* don't believe it. But she

takes my outstretched hand.

'What?' she says, ready to pull me to my feet. Her movement catches a sensor and the garden floods with light.

'No,' I groan, covering my eyes with my hand. Ali comes to my side. Squinches up close to me so the light clicks off.

'Headache,' I say.

'Looking for sympathy, Hennessy?' Ali's voice is mocking, but her hand, not the one I'm still holding but the other hand, comes out of the darkness and rests against my temple. It's cool and kind.

'There, there, there,' whispers Ali Patel. 'Will I kiss it better?'

We don't mention Richard when we go inside. He's there though, like Banquo's ghost, breathing down my neck, when I kiss Ali properly.

'You're a bad boy, Danny,' Ali tells me when I'm leaving. She whispers because we heard a car coming and thought it was her folks.

The car parks across the street, however.

Now I know why the Old Boy was preening himself.

'Look, there's your mum, Danny,' says Ali.

As I say, yon writing business wasnae for me. I'd the pencil, the paper, but none of the words. Yet I'm thinking: those lakes and mountains, that sky. I'll never see the likes again. So I drew them and that was it. I couldnae stop.

Rosie asked, was I the full shilling when I wrote her for a paint box and a proper sketch pad. Thought I was having a joke, that the picture of a snowy mountain I sent her was done by someone else. *Is it no' house paint you want, Dan?* she wrote me back.

But already I was moving up in the world with my sketches, some of the officers getting wind of what I could do. One morning our colonel sent for me. Thought I was in for trouble, but no. He wanted me to sketch a lake, seven or eight miles from barracks. Sent me off for a day. And he paid me half a crown. More than Rosie's paint box cost.

The Japs took my sketchbook off me at first camp. You'd to empty out your kit, and let the guards poke through it while you stood to attention. Couldnae see what they were doing with your stuff unless they pointed and made you show them what it was or how it worked. You were in bother if you'd too many books, or a compass. Even a musical instrument. If the guards werenae happy with your explanation about something, you'd be skelped around the head till you made yourself clear. Tom Merry had a musical box he picked up in Calcutta. Bought it for his wee lassie. You wound it up and it tinkled 'My Love is like a red, red rose', faster and faster the quicker you turned the handle. It belonged to home, I'd think, whenever Tom played it. And he played it all the time. Part of me wished he wouldnae because it had me yearning for everything I was missing, yet I wanted him to play it because it brought me closer to those things, even if it was only the pain of being without them. Tom must have felt the same. We all would, though none of us would say. You'd sense a pause whenever the tune played and let a chink of our old lives peep through the heat of the day.

Canny say how wrong that tune sounded when Fat

Guard turned the handle. It was like the song had gone sour. He ripped the box apart, smashing it with his rifle butt, looking for compartments that were never there. Caught Tom in the belly with the same rifle butt, so he fell to his knees, landing on the broken pieces of the musical box.

Then it was my turn.

23
JUST VISITING

Crikey Mikey. Neither hide nor hair of my Old Dear since I did a runner from Gubby's office a week past, yet she's like a ferret to a trouser leg the second she claps eyes on me.

'Where've *you* been, Danny?' That's rich, coming from the runaway mum, isn't it?

'Out.'

I know. I know. What would it cost to answer in a civil tongue, instead of being thrawn? But I can't help myself.

'Out where?'

'Just out. Where've *you* been?'

I don't plan that last question. It shoots from my mouth so viciously that it makes my cheeks burn and my eyes water. Scorches the Old Dear too, forcing her to suck air through her teeth like you do when you touch something hot. Before she replies, the Old Boy steps between us.

'Your mother asked you a question, son.'

Ouch. Suddenly my Old Boy's a paid-up member of the Let's-be-on-Danny's-back Club. When he calls me *son* again I feel so ickle that I tell the truth.

'Skateboarding with Ali Patel.'

The wave of relief that swells from my folks is enough to wash me out the room.

'We don't want you going *anywhere* from now on unless you ask first. Get that clear, son? *Get that clear, son?*'

Although my Old Boy's voice, when he repeats himself, is barely louder than a whisper, it puts the wind up me more than any of my Old Dear's banshee threats.

'Yeah,' I mutter reluctantly.

'Yeah what?'

'Yeah, Dad.'

'Better, son. Now get to bed.'

''Night, Danny. Love you,' calls the Old Dear after me, her voice so small that it's easy to pretend I don't hear.

In bed I try to lullaby myself with my Old Boy's latest warning: *'We don't want you going anywhere,'* wondering if his choice of pronoun means my folks are back together. The possibility makes my head pound through sweaty half-sleep. *Please. Please. Please . . .*

The house is still and black when, hours later, I stumble to the bog for a painkiller, old habit making me pause at Grampa Dan's door.

Don't worry, Grampa. Only me, I used to whisper on nights like this, always ready to slip in beside him sooner than face the shadows of my own bedroom. 'Coorie up, Danny,' he'd say if he was awake, pulling his bedcovers back when he saw me in the doorway.

Coorie up, Danny. As if I'm lying beside him, Grampa's voice enfolds me like a hug when I open his door and creep to his bedside. My memory of him lying there is so powerful that I'm unsurprised at first to see a body in the bed. It's only when I realise it's my Old Boy's that I cry out. Never before have I noticed how much he looks like Grampa Dan.

A spear of lamplight from the curtainless window reveals contours concealed by day, as though the flesh of my Old Boy's face has always encased another. His night face is shaped by shadows: pooling deep beneath the sockets of his eyes, framing the white oval swell of his eyelids. His cheekbones rise like a delta from the deepest shadow of all, where the face caves in against the back teeth. Grampa Dan's teeth were never in his face at night

213

and his cheeks would disappear in a puckered row around his gums until morning when he reached in a glass for his smile. These were the only parts of Grampa where flesh was spare. Elsewhere his skin was stretched across his skeleton like cling film. Shiny-smooth in places: in the dip where the eyebrow tailed away. On the tip of his nose. Smoother, whiter than the pearliest pebble you could find on the beach. You'd never think the features on someone as old could be beautiful: soft and smooth, and warm and strokeable, but believe me, sometimes I couldn't help reaching out . . .

Like I'm doing now, searching for the Grampa Dan in my Old Boy's face. 'Danny! Jeezo. What's the matter?'

Soon as he sits up, my Old Boy's Grampa Dan-ness fades. His cheeks plump out. His chin droops. His breath stinks of sleep.

'Why are you in here?' I hiss.

'Shhh!' says the Old Boy, pointing across the landing.

In my folks' bedroom, my Old Dear's clothes sit ever so neatly folded on the chair where she used to pile them, her shoes paired beside her handbag. Like she doesn't live here any more. Like everything about her's just visiting.

24
VIBES

Eight o'clock next morning the Old Boy wakes me. He's carrying a tray: three mugs of tea. The house reeks of burnt toast.

'Rise and shine the working boy,' he chirrups, disappearing into his own bedroom and closing the door. When I leave for my first day at Vibes it's still shut. No sound inside. Is that a good sign or a bad one?

'See ya,' I say to the door. There's no way I'm going in.

'No singles, no boy bands, no chart. Absolutely no jazz.'

Huck's long frame judders like a struck lightning rod. 'Apart from that, Danny, you'll get anything in here. If a customer wants to try a record out at home for a couple of days, get a deposit. Herbal tea, if you're having one. That's it.'

Huck dons his headphones like an astronaut heading to Mars on the rocket ship King Crimson. I'm on my own.

Vibes opens at ten, but by noon my only customer is an old biddy looking for the Post Office. Around lunchtime, Vibes' more typical clientele drifts in like a procession of clones. Every customer is male, on the wrong side of forty, kitted out at the same Black Leather Jacket Emporium. These identikit musos sidle round the music shelves reverentially, propping albums against their real-ale paunches, studying sleevenotes as though they're reading runes. There's something religious about the whole vibe in Vibes. Everybody whispers for a start, and there are almost no sales, although by five, when Huck should be pulling the shutters down, Vibes is jumping. There are dozens of bleary, balding blokes in creaky leather cramming the narrow aisles of the shop, heads buried in gatefold sleeves. I swear some of them have been here all afternoon.

I shouldn't really be surprised when I spot my Old Boy weaving his way through the throng to reach me.

'How'd it go, son?' There's a watermelon grin splitting my Old Boy's face, his voice louder than any other customer. It's obvious that my Old Boy's well proud of me working here: *Look, guys. Huck's given my son a job*. Probably even thinking this is the start of a new phase for his prodigal son. Time to kill the fatted calf and celebrate.

'Well, is the working man hungry? Fancy a burger on the way home?' my Old Boy asks me.

Saddo.

I can read him like a book. Aren't all parents like that? You do one thing that makes them think they've got you back on the straight and narrow, and they act so sickeningly *grateful* and *relieved* that you just wanna piss them off all over again.

'Burger? Nuh!'

'C'mon, Danny. I'll treat you. Huck's not going to mind if I sneak you out.'

I didn't realise that Huck had returned to the planet Vibe until the Old Boy, trying to be cool, winked and – double-cringeville – clicked his tongue at Huck over my shoulder.

'Sure. Split, Dan,' says Huck, lifting the counter to let me pass into the shop. 'You did good. Pick out an album for yourself, and I'll catch you next Saturday.'

Huck stretches, shooing me into the depths of the shop with a sleepy wave of his hand.

'Make it something I like, because this time I'll be

nicking it from *you*, Danny,' the Old Boy calls after me. *Sooo* witty.

I wander among Huck's shelves, reading the vertical spines of records I haven't heard of, or which my Old Boy already has. I wouldn't know what to choose.

From Huck's counter I hear my Old Boy laugh and sing something in a *ning ning* voice that's meant to sound like a guitar.

Sit and have a burger with *you*, ya sac? I think. No chance.

I slip from Vibes back into the real world.

Where you be? Where you be?

This wee Jap fella, half my height, had to stand on tiptoes to bring my sketchbook up to my eye level. He screamed into my face, rapping his knuckles so hard on the pages that the charcoal stained them black. My sketches were so close they blurred: the snow-capped mountain, a lake full of soldiers swimming, a forest landscape from a train.

Where? Where?

I told the guard I didnae have a clue where. Beyond the realms of anything I ever thought I'd see. Which is why I'd sketched them in the first place.

I did try to get the truth across, but as I say: me and words. I was confused enough with my capture, so I shrugged out a few names of stations I half-remembered. Think that's where they were, but I canny mind for sure, I told them. Course that was the wrong way to go about things. Japs didnae take to you shrugging. Made you less of a soldier in their eyes.

I was frogmarched off to meet Fat Guard, part of me thinking this was all a misunderstanding. But I wasnae laughing when every drawing was torn out my sketchbook.

Where this? Why you draw this?

Useless at remembering I was, even when Fat Guard was taking his hand off the back of my head to jog my mind. Lucky he decided I was useless an' all when he came to the sketches of my unit lazing in barracks at Calcutta.

Who this man sleep? And this man swim? Name!

I never gave anyone away, Richard. Acted daft. Even had the wit to make up phoney names when a likeness was too good. By the time the guards marched in Sammy Orr to quiz him on his poetry I was tearing up my landscapes and burning them at Fat Guard's feet. Sammy was witness to Fat Guard stamping my hand over the smouldering scraps of my drawings and pressing down.

No more draw, he told me.

25
JUST LIKE OLD TIMES – REVISITED

'Long time, no see, Danny-Boy.'

Wouldn't it be great if you had a fast rewind facility on your life, so you could press the stop button, go back a bit, do things you've screwed up differently?

Soon as I hear Jakey's voice on the street behind me, I know I should be leaving Vibes with the Old Boy, tholing his dad-chat, scoffing the burger I could have murdered anyway . . .

Instead I end up in the chippy, watching Jakey mulch a fish supper, my own appetite draining faster than water down a plughole.

'C'mon,' Jakey splutters at me, jerking his head towards the street. It's not an invitation.

Jakey walks, his body lurching from side to side like all his joints need oiling. I know he exaggerates this gait because it makes him look even more wide and menacing than he is already. People end up knocking into him through no fault of their own. He just loves that: 'Oi, watchit, ya tube!'

As we head for the park, Jakey barks questions at me.

'What you been up to?

'You've not been up to the den for days. Too good for us this weather?

'Why d'your Old Man leave a message on our machine? Hasslin' my mother. Just as well for you I scrubbed it, Danny-Boy.'

If I don't answer, Jakey stops dead so I ram into the back of him. For this I earn a swift doosh in the ribs. I wish I'd the bottle to hang back, leaving Jakey talking to himself like the nutter he is. Instead, I trot meekly in his wake to the offie nearest the park.

'Where d'you find *him*, Jakey?' scowls Waz when he clocks me. 'See what crawled back,' he nudges Sean, who's busy jabbing through the window at a shabby-looking bloke inside mouthing, 'Merrydown, y'alky; not Babycham.'

Sean turns. Spits at my feet. 'He's not getting any of our bevvy,' he says, watching the shabby bloke leave the shop. Quickly, Sean snatches the plastic bag the man's holding and legs it towards the park.

'Gie's m' two cans, ye wee shite!' shabby bloke wails, making a shoogly attempt to give chase. Arms spread beseechingly towards Jakey, he wails, 'Two cans he promised me.'

'Too bad,' sneers Jakey, shouldering shabby bloke aside. This time Jakey runs me ahead of him into the park, keeping a tight grip on my shoulder until we're up the quiet hill at his hangout.

'Aw, man, Hennessy's no' still here, is he?'

Slugging from a can, Sean glowers down from the top of the hill.

'Actually, guys, I can't stay, anyway –' I begin, trying to sound casual. Even risk a few steps downhill.

No chance.

I'm staying put as far as Jakey's concerned. This is the chemistry he likes: it flexes his leadership.

'Why can't you stay, Danny-Boy?'

'Doing something,' I lie.

'What? Got yourself a date?'

'Maybe,' I mutter as Waz snorts disbelievingly.

'She blind?' quips Sean, groping the air in front of him.

Waz is ready to chip in something else, but Jakey silences him with a glare. 'Since we're your mates, we better meet your date, Danny-Boy. Gie her the once-over,' he says, and pulls out a mobile. Shoves it into my hands. 'Tell her to meet you here, right?'

Jakey's eyes bore into me, watching my finger tremble as I punch buttons on the mobile. His own fingers snap at Sean until he passes over a can of cider. Jakey opens the can and shoves it into my chest, despite Sean's indignant tut.

'Och, Danny-Boy needs loosening up the night,' Jakey winks. 'Seems awfy tense.' His unsmiling smile spreads across his face.

Jakey's smile. Deadly dead it is: all teeth, cold eyes. Turned full on me while he finger-snaps for all the cider cans to be passed over. One by one, Jakey shakes them up and opens them in my face. I'm drenched in spray, cider stinging my eyes and fizzing down my cheeks in sticky tears, much to the amusement of Jakey's lovely assistants. On his bidding, they forage out half-bottles of vodka and gin, and Jakey gets Sean to top up the cans.

'Cocktail party, eh Danny-Boy? Just like old times,' he says, giving me that neck lock I hate, and his knuckle-rub against my nose. I don't remember him pressing so hard before. I taste blood running down the back of my throat.

'Your burd better get a jazz on, Danny-Boy,' Jakey smiles, 'or we'll think she's not coming. That you lied to us.'

It's amazing the things you keep discovering about yourself on life's crooked pathway. For example, I never knew, till Jakey started prowling around me in a circle tonight, that I'm neurologically challenged: that my fight-or-flight survival reflex is busted. Otherwise why the hell would I be stood standing here when I could be doing the hundred metre dash home?

I don't fight either.

Waz and Sean are less than a jab punch from me, standing slightly higher up the hill. They're bearing down, in cahoots with the fierce evening sun, glowing big and orange behind them, like Grampa Dan's watercolour. It blinds me, so I can't see faces, only silhouettes. Jakey is even closer than Waz and Sean, chest to my shoulder, as he scans the park for my non-existent date. I smell the oiliness of his hair, cider and nicotine on his breath.

Surrounded, my legs have taken root, all the fear in my head plummeting like a lift with a broken cable to my bladder, overwhelming me with the desperate need to pee.

At times like this, there's only one thing you can do. Call on the Big Chief and hope he's not at it when he says he's All-Forgiving.

God, let me have dialled Richard's number correctly. Let us pray that he gets my message, and overlooks the fact that I have pinched his girlfriend. Amen.

It's funny, Richard. After the guards took my sketchbook, buggered hand or not, I drew on anything I could get. Toilet paper, mainly, or cigarette packets. Hopeless'd save me food wrappers, and other lads'd loan me books to scribble in. There must be plenty Bibles made it home with my sketches all over the verses: *Love God. And love thy neighbour as thyself.*

I went through Sammy Orr's Bible to find those words after they murdered him. Drew one version of what I'd witnessed there. Sweet Jesus, it didnae make me feel better, though I wasnae drawing to purge myself. That would have been a neat trick: draw and forget. No. I drew it for witness. To say THIS happened. I was there. I saw it, and what I saw'll never leave me.

Richard, I'm done in, going back, turning memory into words. What I'm telling you's always been in my head, but never explained. Just a big tangle of fear and misery that should never happen to anyone. Maybe every man living on after what we went through has pictures in his head like mine. Brighter than the brightest film. Too bright, like you've set the colour wrong and you want to look away because the dazzle hurts your eyes. But you canny; just have to wait till everything dims a bit, though it never goes for good. You get flashes. One minute I'm looking at the telly, the next my head's bursting wi' rows of raggedy skeletons lifting picks heavier than themselves. Bringing them down one after the other after the other from head height to earth. I still hear yon flat, hollow crack – not quite a clean note – of pick on stone echoing up a line of prisoners far as the eye can see. I swear that rhythm's hacked into my skull: the melody of weak men worked to death. I can smell, too. Fresh sweat on top of yesterday's old dirt mingled with the stink – you've never smelt the like – of jungle mud and dysenteric shit from the latrine pits.

Look at me here: clean, washed, hair combed nice. An old man, head teeming wi' the poison of the past. Sound like I've lost my mind. Chance would be a fine thing.

26
JAKEY'S PICK'N'MIX PARTY

'Liar, Danny-Boy,' Jakey says. 'We've waited an hour. You're not meeting anyone.' When he slams against my side, I go down like a felled tree.

'Who did you phone?' he growls, yanking me up by the scuff, only to fling me back on to the grass. I can't answer. I think my lungs have exploded in my rib cage.

'Who did you phone, liar?'

Jakey shoves my head against the ground with the flat of his hand. The impact convinces me that I can never tell Jakey the truth; that it was Richard's number I dialled, pretending I was talking to Ali. When Jakey kicks hard against my groin, I know at least I've done one decent thing, because now he's shouting: 'Was it Dicky-Head? Answer me! ANSWER me!'

'No, Jakey. My mum,' I cry out my lie, rolling into a ball against a welter of kicks from every angle now.

'Mama, Mama, Mama,' Waz and Sean taunt.

'Yer who?'

The kicks are still being aimed, but they're not meeting target. Jakey's holding the others back.

'No way, Danny-boy.'

'Phoned my Old Dear,' I splutter, wishing with all my heart I'd a spell to magic her here now. *My mum.*

'*That* old cow,' says Jakey, smiling his cold smile. '*She* won't be comin'.'

'Gubby's bird, ye mean,' says Sean. Above me, he pumps his pelvis. 'She'll be udder-wise engaged. Geddit. *COW. Udder*-wise.'

Jakey skites his hand off Sean's ear, killing his first ever pun.

'Away you go and find her, Danny-Boy,' says Jakey, stepping back from me.

I don't believe it. Neither do Waz and Sean. Both gesture dumbly, first at me and then at Jakey as if to say: *we were only getting warmed up here. What's the game?*

But this is the game. I am the game.

Jakey watches me struggle from all fours to my feet. With both thighs stouning from a brace of dead-legs, I can't bear my own weight. My eyes won't focus, and one of them – I'm too fuddled to tell if it's left or right – feels like it's hanging out its socket; a trophy on a pole. My face feels wet and fat and sticky. There's blood all down my T-shirt. When I press my tongue against the throb in my gum, it pokes through a space where ten minutes back there was a tooth. Jesus! I've never been beaten up before, but I tell you: it's nothing like the movies where you groan a bit, wipe your mouth and walk away. Jakey's assault has damaged all my senses, every inch of me ready to wince at the slightest touch. Yet this is nothing, *nothing*, to the damage that's been done inside my head.

I'm freaked, like an animal caught in a trap, too hurt and weak to fight, yet desperate to get away. They're going to kill me. They don't care. Nobody's going to stop them.

I try again to scramble upright, sobs betraying the measure of my fear. When I'm almost on my feet, Jakey hooks his hand around my neck and draws me down again as if I'm made of cardboard. My face is pressed against cool grass.

'Scared, Danny-Boy?'

Jakey kneels down beside me. He's smiling, his voice soft when he sits back on his haunches, looking to Waz and Sean with a disappointed shrug.

'Easily scared, our Danny-Boy.'

'So what can we do to him now, Jakey?'

Waz downs the last of his cider and lets his can drop. Before it glances off my nose, Jakey deflects it, laying his heavy palm across my face.

'Danny's had enough,' he says, in that kindly voice that scares the crap out of me. 'Let's give him something for the pain, before he runs home to Mummy.'

I wasn't ready for this.

They pin me against the grass – as if I could fight them back – Waz sitting on my legs, Sean holding my head still. Jakey pulls my mouth open. I'm gagging, trying to lock my tongue against its roof, but Jakey prises a gap, and forces several tablets in with splashes of vodka. I feel his rings scraping against my teeth and gums as I gag. When he's done, his fingers are slimy and covered in blood. My blood.

'Manky,' he says, wiping himself on my T-shirt. He pushes Waz aside and takes his place on my shins.

'What d'you give him?' asks Sean.

'Think it's morphine.'

Think?

My head screams. I daren't speak, though. If I speak I might swallow.

'Look at him, scared shitless, man,' laughs Waz in my face.

'You buy from Ming?' asks Sean. Jakey nods. 'Gave us a pick 'n' mix. Six left. Danny-Boy here's had four.'

'Four? Big o' you, Jakey,' Waz says, daringly snide.

Four, I'm thinking. Je-sus. Four of what? Jakey's holding out his palm. 'Here's what's left. That blue one's a jelly. There were two of them. That looks like E.'

'That's a Haliborange.'

Waz lunges, swallowing an orange pill before Jakey can stop him. The other tablets scatter around me.

'Oi! Careful. These cost thirty quid.'

I'm ignored, Jakey and the others scrambling after the rolling pills. They're laughing, fighting like weans over who takes what, swigging back what they find with the vodka and gin.

Pick 'n' mix, I'm thinking, struggling to hold whatever I've been forced to take just above my Adam's apple. It's burning my throat, a vile, sour taste mixed with vodka. I'm desperate to swallow. I mustn't, though;

have to get rid of these pills before they enter my bloodstream. How long do I have, I'm thinking. Is it twenty minutes?

Bouncing on my shins, Jakey's hooting stupid about something, the sound of his laughter jerking me back a bit from where I'm starting to drift. Though his full weight's on top of me, I don't feel him any more. I hear Sean some way off.

'Look at him, man,' Jakey shouts. '*He's* pure away wi' it. Trying to speak and he canny.'

Jeez, I'm thinking, I didn't even know I was moving my mouth.

'He's twitching like a spazzy.'

Guffawing, Jakey rolls off me. 'Wasnae a Hali-borange, Waz, eh?' says Sean.

He wasn't talking about me at all.

Relieved of Jakey's bulk, I move gingerly, flexing my toes. They obey. I see Jakey lumber away, caught up in something else. Turning on my side, I sneak my fingers down my throat.

'What's Waz wavin' his arms for? His eyes are poppin'.' Sean's still laughing, but there's a worried catch to his voice. 'Y'all right, Waz? Is he all right, Jakey?'

'Waz? You're kidding us, right?'

One retch, my throat turning inside out, and there are four pills quivering like aliens in a foul mucous membrane, dangling from an umbilical string of saliva. Two pills, small and beige are halfdissolved. The remaining two, one blue, and one that looks exactly like a Haliborange, haven't melted yet.

I'm OK, playing dead so Jakey ignores me. But nearby, Waz is in some state.

He's wheezing, making his chimp noises – unintentionally for once. Jakey doesn't appear to be getting the situation. He's creased double with laughter. 'Ace wind-up, Wazzer. You've got us going.'

However, Sean's freaking now, bawling at Jakey in a right panicky voice, 'What's Waz taken? He canny breathe. I took a blue jelly like him.'

'Cool the beans, wee man. Waz is at it.'

'He needs an ambulance, Jakey.'

'No way.'

'And what about Danny? You gave him a bloody cocktail.'

'What about him? He's moving, in't he?' Jakey's walking downhill backwards as he answers Sean.

Suddenly he turns. And runs, leaving Waz twitching on the grass, doing the dying fly.

Give Sean his due. He doesn't follow Jakey, and he could have done. For what it's worth, he stays. Not that he's much help.

He's retching for Scotland to bring up the blue pill he swallowed. What a racket! When I see the mottled blue-black tinge to Waz's skin I start tugging him down the hill myself until finally Sean grabs his other side. Together, without a word, we slither Waz towards a pathway which leads to a busy area of the park.

'Phone an ambulance,' I tell Sean when we're down. When he hesitates, I muster all my anger and yell: 'NOW.'

In the distance, a couple run towards us. They're calling my name, the girl moving faster than the guy.

I check Waz is still breathing, then leave him in the recovery position for Richard and Ali to find.

Then I do a Jakey and disappear.

I wasnae right in the head when I came home, Richard. Shut everything out. Everyone.

Getting nabbed with my drawings was the last straw for me. Till then, I was coping – if you could call it that. I mean, I wasnae beaten any more than anyone else, and I was subsisting, like everyone else, on the same starvation diet. Rice and fish stock.

I was dying, of course. Twenty-two and winding down like an old clock, knowing it was only a matter of time before I'd go under with beriberi, cholera, typhus, parasites . . . I could have taken my pick of diseases that could finish me. I'd lost Hopeless and Sammy and Taff. Out of my good mates only Tom Merry remained.

Then he went. Scraped his shin carting railway sleepers one day. That was him. A scratch: how's that for a heroic death? See, wounds don't heal when there's no protein in your diet. And it doesnae help if there's no bandages or disinfectant. When you're weak already, the smallest nick can end up a tropical ulcer.

I'm not going to put you off your scoff, Richard. Look up a medical book if you want pictures. I'll just say dying of a tropical ulcer isnae pretty. Or quick.

Our MO – right decent fella – went grovelling to Fat Guard for some antibacterials. Not just for Tom, but for the dozens of men with ulcers. Our war was a coupla years too early for antibiotics. Still, antibacterials, dab of disinfectant, better diet and Tom and the rest might have stood a chance. The MO put it like that to Fat Guard: I'm only saving your workforce, he said. Might as well have howled at the moon.

Tom got septicaemia. It buggered his heart. Japs still had him digging – like Taff – though Tom couldnae put his weight on the bad leg any more. It was that swollen and infected you could see it throbbing. When he collapsed, two guards toted him to the sick tent, dragging his ulcer through the dirt.

I sat with Tom all night. The MO could do nothing but leave me water to feed Tom in spoonfuls. Me 'n' Tom talked about what we'd do after the war. Promised we'd meet in Carlisle, halfway between Glasgow and

Manchester. We'd take the train. Have a bite. Maybe a donner about, then a decent pint and home.

I drew Tom while we talked, feathering out the shape of him on his mat. I knew he was going. There were pools of shadow in the hollow of his eyes. You could see the thread of his pulse beating in the salt cellar between his collarbone and his neck. Poison shining like a light through the skin on his leg.

I drew his ulcer. There were maggots in it. I saw down to the bone.

That's what I was concentrating on drawing when Tom's breathing stopped. I looked up, and saw his eyes glazed, turned towards me. Seemed best to keep working, so I did, not knowing the MO was at my back.

'Remarkable work, Corporal,' he told me, and borrowed my picture to show his fellow officers.

27
SQUIRM, SQUIRM . . .

I must be away with the fairies when I wake in Grampa Dan's bed God knows how many hours after I limped home from the park and collapsed into my Old Boy's arms. It's so dark in Grampa's room the streetlight blasts my eyes like a laser. I was dreaming it was the sun frazzling my face while I was stretched out on a patch of ground, arms and legs tied to wooden stakes. I'd been there for hours, I thought, hearing my own skin singe and crackle and cook.

Then the moan of someone in a pretty bad way escapes my mouth, triggering pain receptors in my throat I didn't know I have. It must be swollen because, when I gulp, I feel I'm choking. That's when I panic, open my eyes and realise I'm not tied to the ground. I'm home. Pinned to Grampa Dan's mattress, not by stakes, but by blankets.

'Shhh, Danny.'

'Quiet now.'

They're both here, Old Dear and Old Boy, leaning in towards me; sentries on either side of the Berlin Wall. The Old Dear's stroking my forehead the way she used to soothe me to sleep each night when I was wee, and my Old Boy's hand cups my shoulder as if he's shielding me from something. However, every few seconds he squeezes, right on a bruise, as though his fingers can't resist the urge get a dig in.

'What time is it?' I croak, my voice thick. Words taste of blood.

'Shh. Late.' Another squeeze from the Old Boy. 'We can get his story now, Susan,' he says over my head.

'Leave it till morning, Paul.' Although my Old Dear's fingers soothe my forehead with the same gentle stroke, there's a hiss of irritation in her voice.

My Old Boy sighs, rising wearily.

'That's right, Paul. Walk away.' My Old Dear's under-her-breath mutter is pitched clear as Highland spring water, making the Old Boy pause in the doorway. He's biting his lip. Head down. For some reason, I'm tempted to call him back. *Stay, Dad. I'm sorry. I'll tell you what happened. Don't go.*

But, too weak to struggle to my elbows, I'm stuck with a Grampa Dan-eyed view of the world: visitors cut off at the thigh. Framed in exit. Forever walking away.

My Old Boy leaves the bedroom, then, unexpectedly, flings Grampa's door open again. *He's coming back to sit beside me*, I cheer inwardly, but – BOOM!

Instead, my Old Boy pulls a pin out of a grenade and chucks it on the bed before I can take cover. 'Sooner the police take a statement from this joker, Susan, the better.'

Before I have to give anyone a statement in the morning, I have a visitor.

'You're a babe,' says Ali Patel. 'Eye's all gunk.'

She's not squeamish, I'll give her that, which is just as well if she's going to be a doctor. She sticks her finger into my mouth to feel the gap where my tooth used to live, and probes enthusiastically at my oozing eye. It looks and feels as if a golf ball's been forced under my lower lid, and I think it's infected. Green and pus-y's usually a sign, isn't it?

Ali sits facing me on the bed. I pin the blankets tight around my hips in case she decides to view the damage to my nether regions. Still wearing my Hogwarts boxers, for God's sake.

'So, what happens now, you daft prat? Going to Borstal?'

Ali leans in close to me, drawing her thigh on to the bed so that it presses against mine. She smells of flowers, I think, watching her lips move kissing close through my good eye.

'I was really worried about you,' Ali whispers. 'I thought you'd taken the same stuff as that loser they took to hospital.'

'Is Waz still in hospital?' I ask, but before Ali answers my Old Dear bursts through the doorway. On active surveillance she is.

'Would you like a cola, Alison?'

You can practically hear her nooky-assessment programme booting up.

Male and female: affirmative.

Heterosexuality quotient: maximum.

Status: unchaperoned.

Location: double bed.

ABORT.

ABORT.

ABORT . . .

'Danny,' my Old Dear smiles coldly, 'you could try to get up now. Alison can wait downstairs till you're dressed.'

Drat and double drat.

I must be in love, because I take a shower before I rejoin Ali. It's the best shower I've ever had. Makes me feel brand new. Grampa Dan always used to say that when, after days of hinting to anyone who came near him, 'Oh, I could fair go a spray,' my Old Boy finally took the hint. Eased Grampa out of bed, and half-zimmered, half-carried him to our bog. My Old Boy would have to wear his swimming togs and stand in the bath holding on to Grampa Dan. The whole process would have been easier if my Old Dear had been able to help too, but Grampa Dan was twitchy about her seeing him in the scud. By the time I was big enough to help, Grampa was too shoogly to shower any more. A nurse came in twice a week to give him a sponge bath. He hated it.

My blood-clagged hair is clean now, eyes looking and feeling much better minus their crusts. I've even cleaned my teeth.

All for nothing.

'Richard came looking for Alison,' says the Old Dear, adding her irresistible refrain: 'Nice boy, that.'

At least my shower means I'm fresh for my next visitors. Two cops from the Drug Squad who tell my folks they can't wait any longer to interview me. After all, I'm not in Intensive Care.

Like Waz.

'Had a bit of a doing there, Daniel,' the first cop says, trained in observation skills that'll see him all the way to Superintendent one day.

'What happened?' cop number two fires at me before I can shape a smart-ass reply. From the sheaf of notes in his hand I'd say he's already in possession of the facts.

What can I say? *Jakey Wilson and his mates beat me up for no reason.* You don't grass up your mates, especially with mates like Jakey.

That's why I blab this cack about falling down a hill in the park. Said I stonked my head off a stone and couldn't remember any more. 'Amnesia.'

This is the same yarn I spun for my folks. They don't believe it either, but everyone lets me keep spinning till I'm well tangled.

I make no mention of Jakey whatsoever, keeping my

black eye fixed on a sticky ring on the coffee table to avoid the disappointed faces of my folks and the beady scrutiny of the cops. What's that line? The eyes are windows to the soul. That might explain why the smarter looking cop sticks two school photographs of Waz and Jakey under mine while I'm describing how I bruise like a peach.

'Recognise these gentlemen, Daniel?'

I nod, barely.

'Now what I can't understand, in the light of all you've told me,' says the smart cop, 'is why this gentleman here,' his fingernail taps Jakey's chin, 'claims you supplied narcotics to this gentleman.' The finger slides to Waz's spotty cheek.

Must be a major downer for anybody's folks: hearing cops accuse their sprog of supplying drugs. Every parent's nightmare. I didn't have to look up once to know that my folks were in shock. You know when you've done something so wrong that it pushes your folks to the limits of – their love, I suppose. If you weren't their flesh and blood they'd wash their hands of you. I reckon my folks have reached that point with me.

See, Waz is on a life-support machine. Touch and go. Whatever he took in the park made his lungs close down.

I get all this from the first cop while the other flicks through a file of mugshots as if he isn't listening. Then he cuts the first cop off by throwing his folder down over Waz and Jakey's photographs, like he's heard enough small talk. The folder lies open at two pages of faces, maybe a couple of dozen. All teenage boys.

'Who do you know here, Daniel?'

Blonde. Ginger. Dark-haired. Long-haired. Skin-headed. Gelled-up. Gelled-down. Earringed. Bearded. Blue-eyed. Brown-eyed. Speccy-eyed. Cross-eyed. Even a one-eyed guy. Each mugshot I scan is different from the next. After all, no two faces are the same?

Right?

And wrong, because the freaky thing isn't that these mugs were all different, but that in many characteristics – the razor-sharp cheekbones and skin the colour of baker's clay, the dull eyes and pinprick pupils – they were, well, *homogeneous* is the right word, isn't it? *Composed of similar or identical parts or elements.* I defined it in my last vocab test for Gubby.

And the reason for homogeneity in all these

individuals might as well have been tattooed on every forehead: druggie.

No wonder the Old Dear clutches at her stomach when I point out the sorriest-looking specimen on the page: Ming. She must be thinking, Why would *my* son know a lad like that?

'Seen him about,' I say.

'Craig Mulholland,' mutters the first cop, pinching his nose shut automatically.

'And when was the last time? Be specific, Daniel.'

Sharp cop fires the question, leaving his sidekick to take down everything I say. Take down and use in evidence.

'Have you ever done business with Craig Mulholland?'

'Who?'

'Ming. Don't come it, Daniel.'

'No.'

'Have you ever been present when anyone else has purchased something from Craig Mulholland?'

'No.'

That's right. I lie.

'No? That's not what Jakey Wilson says,' chimes in first cop, leafing, casual, back though his notes. 'He claims you'd fifty pounds burning a hole in your pocket last week and suggested the pair of you went looking for Craig Mulholland.'

'We've got you outside St Anne's secondary on security camera with Mulholland and Wilson.'

'Jakey Wilson alleges you sold property of your father's to obtain money for drugs.'

'Why did you sell Walter Brown narcotics?'

'Do you realise how serious this is, Daniel?'

Each question the two cops throw has me on the ropes. I want to tell them, *It wasn't me. It was Jakey.* But I daren't incriminate him.

What kind of weed does that make me? Tangling myself in my own yarn, in front of my own parents. Standing over me, side by side, they seem miles apart. My Old Dear, clutching at her stomach, looks so awful I want to tell her to sit down. And my Old Boy, he's beeling with me, I can tell. Neither of them chips in one word to my defence but watch me wriggle and squirm from one lie to the next like a fly on the end of a pin. They must be disgusted.

The MO – Doctor Jackson I mind his name – was impressed by my sketches of Tom Merry on his deathbed. He asked me to draw everyone in the sick tent. As detailed as possible. 'Most helpful, Corporal,' he says, 'if you could note what's caused these soldiers' wounds or sickness.' Doctor Jackson would spell the medical terms out for me, sometimes scribbling in his own notes. He always wanted me to add names. Victims. Perpetrators. Information like that, he said, would be invaluable after the war. I asked for toilet paper to draw on. He saw I had supplies and pencils.

'That's a rare gift you've got, Hennessy,' Doctor Jackson told me. 'You'll have trained at the Glasgow School of Art?'

Aye, that'll be right, I'd have said if it wasnae insubordination, the Glasgow School of Art's full of bread-van drivers.

After the war, Richard, officers could get to university if they fancied – Glasgow School of Art and all, no doubt. Plenty took the chance, and ended up in careers they'd never have had without the war.

Me? Even if I'd been of rank to qualify, I wouldnae have made a student. Couldnae. When I got home it was all I could do to take a donner round the university grounds, never mind study there.

See, they caught me with all the drawings I made after Tom Merry died. There were dozens. Different from anything I'd done before. Incriminating, you'd say, because I sketched *everything* the Japs wouldnae want made public. A day's rations — to scale. The work parties. The sick tent. The tortured — and their torturers. And I'm not blowing off here, Richard; my work was good. True to life, like the way Danny sketches, so you knew who was who and what was what. I could draw from memory an' all, details stored like photos in my nut. Still are. I could draw you anything I saw. If I hadnae been caught. Disabled.

If Fat Guard hadnae seen himself like I saw him.

28
CLEANING OUT MY CLOSET

When I wake of my own accord on the last day of my suspension, I'm daft enough to think, O What A Beautiful Morning! Could this long lie, I wonder, mean my Old Dear's thawing at last? After all, every day this week, since she moved back in (For good? She's not saying and *I'm* not asking.), she's had me out my scratcher an hour earlier than a normal school day, setting me chores to keep me occupied. I've been cleaning out my closet, as another very bad boy says, right down to ripping my Skarrs posters from the walls, and cutting up all my imported band T-shirts for rags, no argy-bargy. To say there's been a prickly aura about my Old Dear is like describing Caravaggio as a decent scribbler. Rub her up the wrong, and she'll detonate. She's seething, but doing it silently, which is bad.

Things between me and my Old Boy are even worse. Hasn't spoken to me – or the Old Dear, as far as I know

– since the cops first came round. Yet the atmosphere chez Hennessy burbles thick with the sound of words unsaid, both my folks on a mission to wise me up the hard way.

Which is why, this morning, I'm surprised I haven't had my usual rude awakening. Maybe, I think, it's because it was so late last night when the Drug Squad cops finally brushed their shortbread crumbs to the carpet and left.

'Now we're getting somewhere, Danny,' the smarter cop said.

I'd finally admitted I knew who beat me up (though I didn't name names) and I corroborated Waz's statement that I didn't give him a pill and tell him it was a Haliborange. The cops also knew it was me who humphed Waz to the main walkway of the park.

That's why I'm getting a lie-in, I decide, yawning my way downstairs. For being a snitch. Maybe someone'll even speak civilly to me today.

'Congratulations,' cheers the Old Boy when I enter the kitchen. He's late for work, I'm thinking, wondering why he's thrown his chair to the floor. He knuckles a letter into my chest on his way out. The Old Dear follows him.

'What next, Danny?' she sighs.

Dear Mr and Mrs Hennessy,

As you know, Daniel is one of several pupils who have been involved in a serious drug-related incident while under suspension from the Academy.

Due to the gravity of this incident, our Board of Govenors has concluded that there is no longer a place for Daniel at the Academy.

You will appreciate that a decision of this magnitude was not taken lightly. I hope Daniel can be placed in a school where his potential might be channelled without distraction.

Yours sincerely,

Dr Ethel Love

Headteacher

'Grampa Dan, look.'

'In the name of the wee man, who's this?'

'It's me. Danny.'

'That's never my Danny all dressed up like that.'

'Gram-PA. It's me. In my new uniform.'

'Och, you're a wee smasher in that blazer. Here. Some pennies to hansel your pockets.'

'Four pounds! Thanks, Grampa!'

'See and make us all proud, Danny.'

Neither of my folks comes near me. I sit at the kitchen table, reading and rereading the Love Doc's words, hoping they finally unjumble: We can't wait to see Danny back at school on Monday. OK, I know I give the impression that school sucks, but some bits are passable: art, English, art, music, art, circle time, art . . .

Now I'm expelled. *Terrible stigma.*

That's one of phrases I hear the Old Dear ranting at my Old Boy. And the rest:

I've really had it with him.

He's no respect for anyone.

Never lifts a finger, expecting everything to be handed to him on a plate.

Look at his hair.

Look at his clothes.

Look at those morons he hangs about with.

Etcetera, etcetera, etcetera as the King of Siam would say.

Usually I mouth whatever my Old Dear's on about back to myself in the mirror for a laugh, but today I can't. I wince, because I know everything she says is true: I have let her down.

I'm a vomit.

That's how the Old Boy sums me up. On the phone to Gubby.

'Complete vomit. I'm sorry to say it, Mr Gubbins, but it's fact. Susan's in a terrible state. I can't talk to her. How's Danny? I couldn't care less. No . . . don't apologise, Mr Gubbins, but yes, I'd appreciate coming in to see you now. Can't face my own students today anyway.'

My Old Boy's been away all day, leaving the Old Dear home. Her downstairs, me in my bare-walled room. Our phone rang twice, but neither of us answered. I thought about it, hesitating at the top of the stairs, but I couldn't go down. It felt as if invisible briars had sprouted across the stairs. A spell cast: Do anything in this house again, and you die. Neither of us went near the kitchen, which explains why I smell the fish suppers the Old Boy brings home when he's halfway up our road. You could never be an undercover chip.

'Dinner,' he hollers.

Although I'm starving, my stomach clenches in spasm over every mouthful I swallow. There's nothing to drink with the grub, but I don't feel it's my place to run myself a glass of water. When my Old Dear picks up a chip, drops it on her plate and leaves the room, the Old Boy tips her meal over his own and eats noisily, both hands stuffing his mouth. He washes down his dinner with Guinness. First time I've ever seen him drink from a can at the table.

I chew politely, gagging silently when I land a bone. My meal tastes of cardboard, but I daren't leave any of it. Normally it would be no big deal. Old Boy use to say at mealtimes, 'See when I was wee, Danny, your Grampa used to make me eat every scrap on my plate. Even the fat. "We picked crumbs off the dirt in Burma,"' Grampa Dan'd say. I don't care, I'd think.'

My Old Boy never forced me to finish anything, but I don't fancy playing fussy beggars tonight. Although I'm done, I don't saunter from the table in my usual manner, leaving someone else to clear up after me.

That's what the Old Boy does though, abandoning his greasy wrappers, and empty cans. Doesn't even put the lid back on the ketchup.

'There's an art folder for you,' he says.

Since there's no one else in the room, I presume he's talking to me.

Miss West called the art folder our portfolio. Let us decorate the outside with anything we liked.

'I'm really looking forward to seeing what you design when you're given complete artistic freedom, Danny,' she told me as she gave out huge cardboard covers at the start of term. Seems like a lifetime ago.

'Hey, Miss, we can draw anythin' on this?' Jakey had interrupted her.

'Well, something original that reflects you.'

Jakey covered his folder in skulls and dozens of naked women with huge nipples, ripping off the cover of Skarrs' first CD. I didn't have the brass neck to do the nudies, but I liked the skulls idea, so I did that too.

When Miss West, moving her silent way around the

class, stopped at Jakey's folder, she turned chalk white.

Jakey held his red pen delicately, like a paintbrush, as he coloured in a pair of boobs. He twiddled an imaginary moustache.

'Classy, eh, Miss?'

'Original, I said,' Miss West muttered. And while Jakey spent the rest of double art explaining his design to the Love Doc, I changed my skulls to roses.

I'm well proud of this folder. Glad I got it home, though I'd rather it was still in the art room. I gave everything in here one hundred per cent plus, and it shows. I'm not being cocky when I say that, just honest. I gave everything my full attention. Even the pieces I didn't enjoy doing so much, like textile work, where I knitted Jakey's face – *That you making a new pal, Danny-Boy?* I was so into art at the Academy, I'd have gladly come in at weekends to work away by myself.

Graphics. That was ace. I worked on a concept for Skarrs' second album, *Suffering Songs*, using a skull as the focal point and drawing my interpretation of the lyrics around it. I'd black and white photos of real prisoners of war herded in the eye sockets, and I gave the skull barbed-wire eyelashes made out of knotted thread sprayed silver. I put a red felt scar down the cheekbone of the skull and rolled up shredded kitchen paper to look like maggots poking out of it. The background was painted in different tones of red to represent blood drying.

I burned on the skull's forehead with a match.

Miss West said that although my work deserved an A star for effort, my chosen subject matter was vile and inappropriate.

'You should have known that, Danny. Take it home,' she said, 'and do me a concept based on Romeo and Juliet instead.'

My Capulet vs Montague boxing poster silkscreen might have been a contender for the art prize this summer, not that disgraced former pupils qualify. I hang it over the punky rips on my wallpaper, made when I tore my Skarrs posters down.

As I shake it out, an envelope flutters to the floor.

Danny, Miss West writes,

> *I'm really sorry to be losing you from my class. Teaching a pupil with your talent has been a privilege for me. Please don't waste it when you go to St Anne's. Matt Sillers, head of art's my friend. I'll be telling him all about you!*
>
> *Choose your friends more wisely, Danny.*
>
> *Good luck,*
>
> *Miss West*
>
> *PS – I've photocopied your last drawing. Sorry about the quality. The original's in a competition I entered for you.*

I find the photocopy Miss West mentions: my life drawing. Even though it's unfinished, I have to admit I'm well impressed with my effort. There's Posh Guru draped across the art room chairs, looking out at me, as lifelike as any charcoal sketch could get. Posh Guru's body and Grampa Dan's face. Because of the quality of the photocopy, dark areas, like the hollows under the ribcage and the dips in the cheekbone, are more grainy and pitted than the original, enhancing the contrast between light and shade. It's so good I pin it up on my wall where Seth Lamprey in his SS uniform used to give me the Skarrs salute. It's next to my blood-red prisoner of war skull.

They don't go together. Funny how it takes a fresh eye to notice things you've accepted without question. The subtleties in the life drawing make the red paintwork of the skull picture look like something I splashed on blindfold. The barbed wire, fencing prisoners in the eye sockets, is clumsy compared to the way I've draped the loincloth over Posh Guru's privates. I tear down the skull and bin it.

The first drawing Fat Guard grabbed showed his hand yanking back the head of a man kneeling at his feet. Other hand swiping his sword through the man's trunk.

This was a record of something that happened earlier the same day Tom Merry died. Fella we called Sneak was the one on his knees. No idea what he'd done. Till then most of us thought he was in with the guards. Sammy Orr warned me way back to watch when Sneak was about. Not to let on if anything in my kit shouldnae be there. There was a story that in his first camp, Sneak worked a plan to escape. Except he didnae go with the other lads. They were caught. Run through. He went on light duties.

Today Sneak was slaughtered on the edge of the latrines. When I saw him marched through camp, I followed. Heard him begging for his life, hands clasped up to Fat Guard's face. He was pushed to the ground, disembowelled – still alive – then beheaded. All Fat Guard's work. He sweated lard at the effort, his sidekicks watching. One of them retched when Sneak's head fell and Fat Guard kicked it like you would a stone. Sneak's lips were moving though his head was severed, nerves still twitching.

So that night I drew. The kicks. Sneak's dead lips talking. Disgust of the guard who wasnae happy being there, God bless him.

And Fat Guard's pleasure in the killing.

Drawing, I'd get lost in myself, that keen to make everything true on paper while details were fresh, and there was light to see. You'd think my head was wired to my pencil because I'd forget I was hungry, and scared and homesick. Even the pain of sitting on the bones of my arse would be gone. All that mattered was my duty of recollection. A privilege. Everything else was nothin'.

Daftie, eh? Thinking I'd be all right at the back of the hut with my back to the door? Plenty of time before they reached me, to quit drawing and start reading my Bible. I'd have my head buried in scripture, underlining all those holy words with my sketching pencil.

'Guard me, O Lord, from the hands of the wicked, preserve me from violent men.'

I was that caught up, getting Fat Guard's expression right, that I was face to the floor before I knew what was what. Me and my Bible both, all my toilet paper pictures fluttering round my ears.

To this day I don't know how they caught me. Reckon they found some sketches I'd done for Doctor Jackson. My initials were on them.

All I know is that Fat Guard had his sentries laying into me while he went through my artwork. He shrieked in my face, shaking a fist stuffed with toilet paper at me while I was kicked and pistol-whipped. No one else in our hut was searched. There was this background silence that roared like the sea when you clamp a shell to your ear. It softened the blows and kicks and cracks to flesh and bone. My flesh and bone. Every man stood and gave the salute when I was dragged outside. Matchstick men. Last time I saw any of them.

29
BOOTING UP

I never thought I'd hear myself say this, but today I've been grateful for my Saturday job in Vibes. It's given me a chance to defrost after the return of the Ice Age triggered by the Love Doc's death warrant. Glacial, it's been at home all week; the Old Boy waking me this morning with a cold flannel and silence instead of a cuppa like last Saturday. Brrrr.

Which is why I'm hardly ecstatic to hear his voice at closing time in Vibes.

'Don't tell me Danny's left already, Huck?'

Left? I've barely had a comfort stop since the working day began with me humping twenty-five computer boxes down Vibes' skinny basement stairs into the bowels of the shop.

'Twenty-first-century technology, man,' Huck had gestured helplessly at the boxes when I squeezed in for work round his unpacked hard drive. Close to tears, he

266

said, 'Sort this for me, man, and you've paid your dues.'

An offer I couldn't refuse. Although it's taken all day, I actually succeed in getting Huck's new system to power up and bleep. What's more, the task has filled my mind so completely that there's been no pondering room for what a suck my life is. In fact – whisper it – the day's been a blast.

Until now, that is, when I hear my Old Boy's dulcet tones as I'm booting down.

'I don't see him, Huck,' he calls, the pathetic bleat of disappointment in his voice shrivelling the swell of pleasure inside me. Setting it hard as stone.

'I am so here,' I say, crabbit behind a wall of empty cardboard. *You've broken the spell that's kept me feeling good all day. Now I feel knackered, hungry, thirsty, grubby . . .*

'Whoa! You've been busy, Danny.' The Old Boy can't hide his relief at finding me, stumbling through boxes to breathe down my neck at the monitor. 'What you doing, son?'

'D'oh? What's it look like?'

I know, I know. I *should* know better, but I can't help myself. My Old Boy's so obviously impressed at seeing me do something constructive for once that he starts throwing all these stupid I'm-a-computer-virgin questions at me as if he's my pal.

'How on earth did you figure all this yourself, Danny? I wouldn't have a clue.'

I could tell him we get ICT twice a week in school, but I don't. Instead I switch off the monitor while he's trying to get the mouse to go where he wants it. I leave him sweating that he's touched something he shouldn't have.

'. . . er, Danny . . . How does this . . .? Ooops, what have I . . .?'

Leave me alone, I drill into his bald patch as I climb Huck's stairs. *Don't try and be nice. You being here's reminded me I'm expelled.*

In bother with the cops.

Grounded so I can't see Ali.

And Jakey's gonna to kill me.

Just piss off, will you?

No such luck. The Old Boy's at my back. 'Wait,' he says, steering me towards Huck. Jolly as Christmas, he lifts one of Huck's headphones away from his ear and announces in this arsewipe of a loud voice: 'Whizzkid here's got your new baby going!'

'Thanks, Danny,' says Huck, with an unenthusiastic

shrug. He swings his plaits dolefully from side to side. 'Now I've to start a database for online orders.'

'Danny'll do it!' My Old Boy volunteers me, the bloody liberty of him! If he'd only waited two seconds, I might have offered to help Huck off my own bat.

But not now.

After embarrassing me like that in front of Huck and his clones, no wonder I'm saying zilch as the Old Boy and myself wait in the pizza shop together. He talks enough for both of us though, his pride at what I've done today making him yatter like a hyperactive budgie, all recent bad history seemingly forgotten. Maybe even forgiven.

I could punch his lights out.

'Come on, Danny, you cyber-star,' my Old Boy nudges me. 'Make a long story short. Tell me all about what you did today.'

If I wasn't already so irked by my Old Boy, hating the way he stands too close to me, I doubt I could speak to him anyway. Having eaten nothing all day, the aroma of melting mozzarella and rising dough makes me weak. I can't take my eyes off my margarita. She's browning far too slowly for my liking.

'Pepper?' the chef asks me, taking my pizza from the oven at last.

'Don't think my computer genius here can wait for pepper,' quips my Old Man, the world's greatest comedian.

That does it.

Him and his stupid, stupid patter.

Before he notices I'm gone, I'm gone.

You willnae have had a doing, Richard? Or Danny. God forbid. You see it on the telly. Folk thumped with fists and baseball bats. They roll about for two minutes and groan. Next thing they're on their feet. Couple of scratches the worse off.

Well, I didnae bounce back. They kicked out my teeth. Broke my ribs, I reckon, not that any medical bod was taking notes. Eyes were so swollen I thought they'd blinded me. They were clever, mind; knew when to stop. Yon expression 'within an inch of your life' – I've been there. They punished me enough so I knew they werenae done with me. Gave me a few hours to recover. A cup of sweet tea. Shoved me under a hosepipe to wash off blood and bring me to my senses. Before they started on me again.

Bang.

Out with the fists. The worry of what they'd do next, when they'd be back, always worse torture than the beatings themselves.

I was questioned – for days probably, though it felt like weeks and months. *Why you draw? Who you spy?*

Here's the best laugh. From my drawings they reckoned I was an undercover agent masquerading as Joe Soldier. Accused me of anti-Japanese activities. Wanted my real rank. Who was pulling my strings? I reckon that's why they kept me alive.

What could I say? I'm no spy. Never wanted to be in your bloody war in the first place. I'm a bread man. A driver. Just want home to hold Rosie in my arms and if I canny go home I want to die. Now. Quick. I'm tired of all this.

But my luck was out. When Fat Guard and his cronies couldnae get anything from me, they punished me worse than death. Or so it felt to me back then when they spared my life and sent me off to Changi jail in Singapore.

On another day, in a different mood, Fat Guard might have shown me mercy. Finished me quick like Sneak. Like Sammy Orr. A few blows, even a few hours of torture, and it'd be over. See, that was one of the worst things about being a prisoner of the Japs: your destiny was random in their hands.

And in their own way, I suppose the Japs did finish me off because before I left camp, they smashed my hand.

30
THE DANGEROUS BROTHERS

Abandoning my Old Boy, I run blindly down the main road.

Talk about cutting off my nose to spite my face. So hungry I could sob, I slump against Woolies' window and watch my Old Boy and his black leather jacket leaving the pizza shop carrying my tea. It would be the easiest thing in the world to catch up with him: *Boo*! *Had you going there, Dad.*

When the security guard from Woolies chaps the window and thumbs me away to a bench in the square, I should take it as a sign. Run after the Old Boy. While I have the chance. But it's too late now.

'Surprise, surprise.'

This sounds melodramatic, but – honest – the sky darkens as a shadow falls.

'Budge up, Danny-Boy.'

Jakey plumps himself down next to me. A larger

figure perches on the arm of the bench on my other side and the tightening of my sphincter tells me it's Nut, Jakey's psycho brother. I wonder if he's got his hunting knife on him.

"Member Danny?' Jakey addresses Nut over my head. Pointedly he adds, 'He's the tube gave Waz the junk last week 'n' blamed me.'

'*That* Danny?' The cogs turn in Nut's bampot brain. 'You were scared to tell the cops about him.' Nut speaks in a monotone, through a mouthful of broken teeth, barely managing to coordinate the actions of talking and poking his finger in my chest.

'I . . . I . . . didn't. I . . .' I stammer, pathetic, staccato, my eyes sweeping the square for the most populated escape route. I don't want my body to lie undiscovered too long.

Not that I'm going anywhere yet. Nut's weight is against me, his arm round the back of my shoulders, pressing me close. Not in any romantic sense, you understand. Think more of a defenceless creature trapped by a beast with a Tic Tac for a brain: Lenny in *Of Mice and Men* with that poor wee mouse.

Jakey has *his* arm across my legs, his elbow digging

hard into one of my quads. I'm boxed in by the Dangerous Brothers. Jakey's eyes, bloodshot, dilated, bore mine. Slowly he speaks: 'We don't want the pigs round our bit again. They noised up my mother. No one does that. Grass me up and you're dead, Danny-Boy.'

'Grass. Dead.' Nut echoes, a million brain cells behind, although, give him his due, he gets the salient points across. I'm hardly going to tease him since I've discovered he *does* have his hunting knife with him. I don't actually see it, but I feel its tip probing the flesh of my crotch through my jeans.

Jakey watches my face, smiling his smileless smile as the knife digs in, his body cloaking Nut's actions from any passer-by daft enough to approach.

'This is your last warning, Danny-Boy.'

Twist.

'If you grass me up, won't just be your goolies missin'.'

Pierce.

With steel poking through denim to my testicles, it's little wonder I hear my own voice snivelling.

'Stop.'

'*Stop*,' chorus the Dangerous Brothers, an octave apart. Weak with laughter, mutually impressed by their impressions of me, they flop across me. Heavy, but off guard. Temporarily, Nut's knife is loose in his hand, flat against my thigh.

'*Stop!*' Jakey mimics me again, loud and shrill. And down Nut's earhole.

'No need to yell, ya wee tube,' yells Nut. With the reflex of a sprinter off the blocks, he fires a punch into Jakey's jaw. At the sight of Nut's fight reflex, my own flight reflex decides to activate for a change. Mustering all the strength I've got, I force the Dangerous Brothers aside. By the time Nut's caught up with the situation, I'm belting for my life across the square.

'You're deid, Hennessy.'

Jakey's threat ricochets from every building around me. Since it's hardly likely to make me rethink my escape strategy, I don't stop till I get to my front door. Of course I've only forgotten my bloody keys, haven't I? With both fists I thump the glass.

'Mum. Dad. Please let me in.'

You canny see the scars on my hands. Not a mark. Look. All the damage is under the skin. Out of sight. Worse, that, somehow. A big scar, a limp, or a leg missing: makes it easier for others to accept. What folk canny see is harder to explain.

I wonder if the Japs knew that.

They took turns to thump down with their heels, one guard pinning my arm flat to give others purchase without the risk of me pulling away. Whenever it was Fat Guard's turn, he laid his swagger stick across my knuckles so my fingers were splayed. Then he squeezed his knees together and bunny-hopped on to me with all his weight. Reminded me of a wean I once saw tormenting a cat. The guard who retched when Sneak was decapitated yelled loudest when he brought his foot down, and never touched me once. I remember that clear, though I didnae stay conscious too long. My pain was white hot, and I reckon it did more damage to my head than my hand. See, somewhere in that torture my brain switched itself off, and I stumbled through the rest of my captivity like a ghost.

And there's my story, Richard.

I told you: nothing brave, nothing special. Surviving. Subsisting. Tens of thousands of blokes making a better job of it than me. You want to find them. Proper soldiers.

In '45 I remember prisoners like that hunting round for uniforms when Changi jail was liberated. Wanting to look tickety-boo when the British MOs parachuted in. These poor blokes could hardly stand. Riddled with every bloody parasite going, legs eaten away by ulcers. Others swollen fatter than barrage balloons with beriberi. And they were trying to give the salute.

Me? I watched our liberation and told myself this was too good. Beyond dreams. If I thought the doc taking up my bad hand, working my fingers gently and splinting my wrist was real, he'd be gone.

But he was real enough. And the orderlies who fed me up and bathed me and cut my hair and stretchered me from truck to train to boat. They were real too.

And so I came home, Richard. A lassie still waiting for me. Just like the talkies.

Rosie.

Lost her before you and Danny were pals.

In the years I was away she hadnae changed, though she looked bonnier in real life than any drawings I made from her picture in my head while we were parted. Same black hair that shone blue, and green eyes that begged me to tell her why I was so different. How could I? It would spoil Rosie for me: her knowing what I'd seen and felt and been. Was hard enough to let her hold me and feel the shake of me, all jag and bone, against her softness, pulling away if she touched my bad hand.

I wasnae right in the head, all these daft things rankling me. I never felt clean, the filth and stench of camp and prison in my nostrils, clinging to my skin. I sickened myself. Sweating through the nights, calling out in my sleep. Waking in my own shit and piss.

I was twenty-four. Worse state than I'm in the now, creeping about in the dark. Lighting fires for water so I could scrub away at myself the nights I couldnae sleep. Jumping if anything creaked, greeting like a bairn if the wind changed. Shunning kindness. Trusting no one.

31
THE TAPE

I wouldn't say Richard exactly welcomes me with open arms, but at least he lets me in.

'Playing chases with your mates again?' Richard eyes the breathless state of me. 'Phone's there if you need to call the cops.'

'I'm locked out. Jakey's brother's after me with a knife. Gonna castrate me –' I begin to explain, but Richard raises his hand and cuts me off.

'Phone's there,' he repeats flatly. 'No good telling *me* any of this, Danny.'

Of course I don't call the cops. Think I'm daft?

I might *look* daft, peeking through Richard's curtains: a nosey wee hing-oot. But I don't phone anyone, and Jakey and Nut don't come after me after all.

Richard keeks his head round the door to say he's too busy to chat.

'Using the kitchen table to spread out my project

while Mum and Dad are out. Why don't you stick the telly on, Danny?' he suggests. 'I don't think your mum 'n' dad'll be late anyway.' And he grins. 'They're away to the pub with mine to talk about you going to St Anne's. Just like old times, eh?'

'Christ, that'll be a wild night!' I snigger automatically before I can stop myself. When Richard flashes me a look – *Plonker* – and leaves me staring at his kitchen door, I wish I'd kept my Jakey-like sarcasm to myself. I've more reason than Richard to remember the great times our folks always had when they got together at our house. We'd get a curry in, and Richard and I would be chased upstairs to watch telly with Grampa. But we never did. Played games instead, perched on either side of Grampa Dan, with dominoes or cards set out on a tray, listening to the bursts of laughter and conversation downstairs, enjoying the exotic waft of spices in the air.

The Old Dear would check us, in between bottles of wine. 'You being a nuisance to Grampa, boys?'

'Away enjoy yourself for a change, Susan. They're a tonic,' he'd say. Richard and I would share a korma. Downstairs. The sight of rice combined with the stink of curry turned Grampa Dan's stomach inside out, he said.

He'd bang down loud for ice cream, though, and the Old Boy would bring up three plates: two piled high with every flavour going, and chocolate flakes and raspberry sauce and wafers poking out. One single ball of vanilla for Grampa Dan.

He could make his ice cream last forever, shaving the thinnest sliver with his spoon and slipping it on his tongue to melt. I'd marvel at his patience, my own ice-cream mountain scoffed in three spoonfuls, ready to get back to the dominoes. But all games were off while Grampa Dan peeled and shaped and savoured his ice cream, as though it was his last meal.

All these uninvited thoughts of curry and ice creams past remind me of my margarita that got away and the fact that I'm ravenous.

Richard won't grudge me a cuppa and a slice of toast, I tell myself. All the same, I hesitate outside his kitchen door. Even raising my hand for a polite sorry-to-disturb-you knock.

And it's just as well I don't barge in. There's a man in there, talking to Richard.

I think my heart recognises the voice before my head and, Jesus, it truly leaps into my mouth with joy before my reason clobbers it back down again. *It can't be Grampa Dan, he's dead.*

But it's Grampa's voice, all right, still talking after I burst in. You'd think he was ignoring me.

Because there's no pause when I throw open the door so violently that it thuds Richard's wall and scuds the side of my head on the rebound. I'd never get away with that round Grampa Dan . . .

BANGBANGBANG. 'What's all that bloody clatter about?' he'd shout.

No interruption as I launch myself at Richard's table, scattering folders and photographs like short-range Frisbees.

BANGBANGBANG. 'A bit less ram-stam, Danny.'

No hesitation, as I hurl myself at the voice I thought I'd never hear again: *GRAMPAAAAAA.*

BANGBANGBANG. 'Hold your wheesht, Danny. I can hear you.'

Grampa Dan's not here though, is he? How could he be? It's months since I took the strain of his coffin-rope myself and lowered him into the ground.

It's a tape; a mini-disc recording.

Though it doesn't stop me jet-propelling myself into Richard's kitchen on a blast of pure hope: *Please be alive. I'll talk to you. I'll listen. I miss you so much. I'm sorry . . .*

Little wonder our Paul, Danny's dad, didnae arrive till I was married six years. Took me that long to thaw out. Rosie was patience itself. She saw I was a shell, rattling with memories, not a real man. Coudnae work. Couldnae drive. Grip a steering wheel. Hold a pen. Tendons were cut, nerves in one hand buggered. And the rest. I saw plenty of doctors.

Some wanted to have a better look. Open up my hands. Aye, that'll be right, I said. No one was getting near me. No one.

Even Paul. My wee son; only son. He learned to keep his distance, knew I couldnae stick him close. Even when Rosie had him swaddled up tight so he couldnae shoogle, I'd hold him at arm's length. The way you would a grenade. Wasnae right. You know yon way wee ones are all over you? I couldnae take it. When our Paul climbed on me, me not knowing what he'd do next, well … it was like going back. Guards coming up from behind, shrieking in my ear. I'd freeze. Lash out sometimes.

The slightest bang had me jumping out my skin, flying off the handle, a bag of nerves, fit for nothing. No chat. No rough and tumble. No football, park, games... We didnae do anything together, our Paul and myself. I'd too much bottled up to let go and play. I'd plan in my head, right enough, what we *could* do , but when it came to the bit...

After a while our Paul knew better than to ask. He'd have had more of a childhood if I'd never come home. Course, that's havering. If I hadnae come home, Paul'd never have been here. Never got to art school.

And there'd be no Danny.

Danny. I was that different with him. He changed me. Brought me back to what I used to be.

He'd be lying there, bonny wee bairn, never the girny sort, still in himself. We'd stare each other out till I was holding him and couldnae recall picking him up. Rosie was alive then, and we were in our own place. Our Paul'd bring Danny down to see his granny and I'd be in my chair at the fire, turned away from the lot of them. Soon as Rosie shooed our Paul out, telling him not to hurry back, I'd have Danny in my arms, just for the holding of him, warm against me. And Rosie, she'd say, 'Mind the bairn for a bit while I clear a path in this house.' She knew fine what the bairn was doing for me.

Danny never wriggled or jerked or cried. He'd bed himself in against me and I'd smell his head, watching him breathe, wishing him the world. He was the unravelling of my pain.

Even when he was bigger, Danny'd coorie up against me. *You're all thin, Grampa.* And the good in him would pass to me, better than any medicine.

He'd get me talking, hungry for stories, and I'd have to rummage for daft things that happened sixty-five, seventy years in the past. Well, I wasnae going to give him my nightmares so I'd to push through them, get behind to reach the way I was once.

And it did me the power of good. Back to being Danny's age. Six to a bed, I'd tell him. Me at the end, falling out every night…

My mother keeping us all shooshed, making shadows on the wall with her hands whenever the rent man knocked at the door.

His favourite story was my adventure when I was five, away off fishing myself for baggy minnows with a jam jar. 'You were allowed out by yourself, Grampa?' I fell in the boating pond in Victoria Park and went under. Nearly drowned. Big posh fella fished me out, wrapped me in his fancy coat, and drove me home in his motor car. My first ever ride. Worth nearly drowning for.

Danny could tell you the story better than I can, he's heard it that often. Used to tick me off if I missed a word out. He never tired of hearing it, and I never tired in the telling. Even after Rosie died and I was numb, Danny kept me going, and even after I ended up stuck here in this room, an old nuisance. You didnae do so bad either, Richard. Rare chat the three of us used to have.

But here, you'll be sick to the back teeth of me havering on and on. Switch that thing off now, Richard and you tell *me* something.

Danny: what's happened to him?

Never comes near these days for me to ask. Aye

stomping past my door and away out. Or playing yon tuneless clap-trap, some fella shouting fit to burst your lugs.

Any news? I say.

Nuh, he goes.

I know he's going through the stages. I was the same at his age. Couldnae be arsed to gee myself with book learning either – though I never cheeked my mother like he does. Thought the best thing that could happen was to get out of school and into work. That would make me a man. Able to stand on my own two feet. Free to serve my country if I was called.

I didnae know any better.

I want things to be different for Danny.

I missed my chances, and I'm not saying that because I'm sorry for myself, or giving it the poormouth. Wouldnae have known opportunity if it kissed me. Nor did my faither, or his faither before him. They were glad enough to be fed and shod and in work.

But look how my odds would have changed if I'd stuck school.

Wouldnae have been low-ranked in the army. Might not have gone in at all. Could have ended up in some protected occupation, never overseas. If I *had* been drafted, and had a bunch of qualifications to my name, even a trade, I might have made an officer. There'd have been perks in that compared to the lot of Joe Soldier: better food, better information. Not forgetting the best perk of all: upping my chances of survival as a better class of cannon fodder.

Don't get me wrong. I'm not saying officers couldnae cop it like the rest of us. Thousands did. As far as the Japs were concerned, a prisoner was a prisoner. But there's no denying captivity was better for officers in general, especially in the early days before every rank was put to work on the railway.

What's any of this to do with my Danny, you must be thinking, Richard, when he's never going to be a soldier, or, God forbid, go through what I went through? Well, I just want him to make the most of his opportunities. *Carpe diem.* Thought I'd get to explain all this myself, but now that he's old enough, he's too old to listen. If everyone was born old we'd know all about bloody *carpe diem*.

How the hell do you know anything when you're fifteen? It was already too late when Doctor Jackson was telling me I could have been a war artist, I'd more talent than anyone he'd seen.

Richard. See Danny gets to know, so he makes the most of himself.

Soon.

Now.

There's no time left for me to tell him what's what. But if he knows all *this*, the state of me won't be a waste.

There's something in this cabinet for him, but he's not been ready to see it. Wouldnae get the point. You mind the key, and when you think it's time . . .

32
SECRETS AND LIES

It's so quiet out here, I can hear the worms fart. I'm
huddled against my back door in the rain, waiting for my
folks to get back from the pub. It's cold, wet, dark, and I
don't care. I could stay out all night. Just me and Grampa
Dan, my head brimming with the sound of his voice,
until the swoop and stretch and slow of Richard's
batteries running down make the words I'm hearing
harder and more horrible to believe.

I've finally done what I'm told for once: talked to
Richard. I think he sussed I'd want to hear Grampa's
story alone, so he made me toasties to go. Lent me a big
puffa jacket. Gave me his mini-disc.

'I'll need the tape back so my project can be assessed,'
Richard apologised. 'Then it's yours. That's what Grampa
Dan wanted. This too,' he said, pressing the key to
Grampa's bedside cabinet into my hand. Not that it's
been much use to me when I'm locked out.

If Jakey had to stand in the rain like this, he'd have our kitchen window panned in, I think, and then I shiver despite Richard's puffa jacket. Because any thought of Jakey tonight leaves a skim of cold sweat on my skin.

Not, as you're probably thinking, because I'm crapping myself about what he'll do next to me, although that *does* put the wind up me slightly. Who wants to join the castrati?

But it's the damage he's done to me already that scares me more.

See, listening to Grampa's tape, I know *I* should have been the one to hear his story first hand. But I couldn't be arsed to listen.

Now I've nothing left but his voice on Richard's headphones. It makes my chest hurt and my throat ache to hear Grampa but not see him.

Jakey has me so damaged that Grampa Dan couldn't show me his scars that never healed. Or tell me about hammering rocks to break them when he could barely lift the hammer. Describe steering rickety wheelbarrows along muddy slopes on the Railway of Death with a precipice below that had already swallowed up two of his pals . . .

What was I doing?

I was singing.

Dancing.

Goosestepping, because Jakey told me to, screaming:

> *We will break you*
> *For your weakness*
> *We will drain you*
> *Till you fall*
> *We will work you*
> *For our greatness*
> *We will kick you*
> *When you crawl.*
> *Kommandant. Kempetai.*
> *Supremacy.*
> *Blow you away . . .*

Grampa Dan used that word: **Kempetai**. Said he wrote it on a drawing hidden in the spine of the Bible he never read:

Kempetai beheads Private Dell for missing tenko. (Reason: in latrines, sick with dysentery.)

How would a dingbat like me know Seth Lamprey was singing in praise of the Japanese military police?

I never gave the words a thought.

I was just copying Jakey.

When my folks finally roll back from the pub, well after closing time, I'm fully primed to dose them with their own nag medicine.

What time d'you call this? Staggering home drunk, having me sitting up for you?

But I don't.

Even if I wasn't too cold to speak, I wouldn't have a go. They're all upset about something, my Old Boy and Richard's folks standing in the road talking in whispers as if they can't bear to make their thoughts any louder than they have to –

'So much blood . . .'

'You wonder if we'd got there sooner, would we . . .?'

'Police said they see it every day –'

'What age? Nineteen.'

'God love him . . .'

Richard's folks, they might as well be one person, so close to each other that their temples fuse. My Old Boy's head meets theirs, but he stares at the ground, keeping a cigarette to his lips. His shoulders are pulled high to his ears same way as when he supervised Grampa Dan's coffin after the funeral. I can't help thinking how good it would be for him if Richard's Old Dear were to reach out, and draw him towards her . . .

Because *my* Old Dear, she couldn't be further from my Old Boy if she flew to Timbuctoo. She's melted into the shadow of our house, sharing the same pool of darkness keeping me hidden. She's hugging herself, sob-shivering. Wild she looks, staggering as if she's three sheets to the wind. Her hair straggles all over her face, sticking to the wetness there: tears and rain. Not that I reckon she cares how she looks. She's ranting away to herself. It's not a pretty sight.

I mean, she's a right old bag at times, I know, but, well, it's not right to see her – my mum – in such a state. That's why I emerge, my arms petrified against my chest from the effort I've made to protect Grampa Dan's tape from the rain.

Pity, that.

Arms can be handy when you're battered by a madwoman.

I kid you not.

The instant she sees me, my Old Dear revokes her fifteen-year no-smacking policy and sets upon me like a prizefighter, pummelling me from all directions. I wouldn't say my Old Dear *physically* hurts me at all: her aim's rubbish, her punches weak. She's blinded by tears. Yet her attack feels worse, much worse than when Jakey and co. were giving me that doing in the park.

'Where have you been?' she rasps, and I swear, her voice is something you only hear from possessed people in horror movies. She looks possessed too, eyes bulging like they're about to pop out on the pavement, all the sinews in her scraggy neck jutting as she strains to launch herself at me again, till my Old Boy and Richard's dad finally pin her back.

It's not funny, any of this. I don't know if it sounds funny. But it's not.

Lights are flicking on in bedrooms. Curtains twitching. Silhouettes appearing in windows. Ali opens her front door – bare legs beneath a long Chillis T-shirt – and when she sees me she looks as if she's coming over before Mr Patel shoos her back to bed. Richard's parents sideslip away.

My Old Dear's oblivious. 'Where have you been?' Her question batters into me, head ramming Grampa Dan's tape against my breast-bone.

'Son, where have you been?' quietly, almost an echo. My Old Boy moves towards me. My Old Dear is sandwiched between us, still swiping her hands against me but without force. She's spent, ready to fall until my Old Boy clasps her shoulders.

'Tell us, Danny.'

My Old Boy's whisper is earnest, his mouth crushed by my Old Dear's head lolling against his face.

'I've been here, Dad,' I say, 'waiting for you.'

And for a change I'm telling the truth.

'You sure you've been here all night, Daniel?'

My folks are not the only people interested in my whereabouts tonight. The sharper of those sharp-suited Drud Squad 'tecs, back in his favourite armchair, asks me the same question. When I sigh, 'Here,' for the umpteeth time, this uniformed bloke he's brought with him stands over me. Legs planted apart, arms folded across his white braided cap, he bears such an air of authority that even my spiral sculpture on the mantelpiece stands to attention.

'Let's not waste time, Daniel,' His voice reverbs to drown the hiss and bleep of his walkie-talkie. 'I need to know your movements.'

Before I can answer him my Old Boy pipes up. 'Superintendent McColl,' he says, 'I've told you already tonight, Danny has *nothing* to do with this. He was here. I picked him up from Vibes record shop. We came home together.'

Now here's a thing, maybe I'm havering from sleep deprivation, but I sense this *firmness* in my Old Boy's manner as he wedges himself in beside me on the settee like he's going to deal with this interview. I have to steal a glance to check it really is him, which it is, though he's not like himself. Jutting chin. Face set. None of his usual woosiness. And he's lying for me. I'm impressed.

'Mr Hennessy.' Not quite so impressed, the Super snaps back, 'Your son must account for himself, so we can eliminate him. Daniel?'

I tell him again: in my garden, locked out. End of story.

Eliminate me, I'm thinking. Eliminate me from what?

'Times, Daniel?' asks Sharp-Suit, licking his pencil.

'Dunno.'

Can't help myself, can I? *Dumb insolence*, my Old Dear would call my attitude. But can you blame me? I don't have a clue why the cops are on my back this time. Christ! All I've done tonight is sit in the rain and listen to a tape. No crime there. Times, they're after, on the one night I lived my Grampa Dan's life. How could I measure his story in common units of time?

'Not good enough, Daniel,' glares Super-Uniform, thumbing Sharp-Suit to his feet. 'Take him to the station.'

'Danny . . .' My Old Boy sounds desperate.

'The Superintendent needs times, Danny,' says Sharp-Suit, sounding equally desperate.

'It's crucial, son. Tell them you were here all night,' interrupts my Old Boy. He's gripping my arm, squeezing it. *Gonna cooperate, Danny*, urge his fingers. 'This is about a . . .'

I don't appreciate the way Superintendent Uniform silences my Old Boy with the threat of a night in the pokey for interfering with their enquiry. That's why I tell them Richard can vouch for me. Right away the Super's on his radio, organising a team to haul Richard out his scratcher. What for? I'm thinking, still trying to figure why the Old Boy covered for me. Something major going down here? I want to ask him, but under the Super's gimlet stare I'm scared my question will unscramble to say what I'm really thinking: this involves Jakey Wilson, doesn't it?

I say nothing. We sit – not the Old Dear, who's meeting Ralph and Huey down the toilet upstairs, but me, the cops, and my Old Boy – in uneasy silence while new morning light creeps over us. Outside, police radios distort the dawn chorus.

When Ali snakes round her front door, making adjustments to her running top, she finds two cops goggling her and jogs off without stretching. I follow her with my eyes until she disappears, straining my neck like the plod who's so busy salivating after her that he trips on his way up my path, dropping the statement he's taken from Richard.

'Let's start again, Daniel.' Superintendent Uniform blasts me with his fatigue-stale breath while he reads Richard's statement. 'Your friend Richard seems to think you came to his door because James and Norman Wilson were chasing you. Is this true?'

I nod – what else can I do? – feeling my Old Boy

shrink into the settee as the Super shoots a rocket up his jaxi for giving me a false alibi.

'Danny, Danny, Danny . . .' my Old Boy starts to keen, head buried in his hands. I feel so bad for him that I make my statement as honest as I can, beginning from when I ditched my Old Boy at the pizza shop. That was wrong, my head screams. Now lay off my dad.

All I have to do then is study a page of knives, picking one with the closest resemblance to Nut's hunting knife. The cops don't hang around after that. They read my statement back to me and thank me for my cooperation. Sharp-Suit shakes my hand.

'You're learning. Ming Mulholland was stabbed tonight,' he says, before he's whisked away with the Super under a flashing blue light.

I press my cheek to the window. Ali jogs back into view, watching the police cars leave our cul-de-sac. Now there's no one but her outside. You'd think nothing had happened.

Except my dad's behind me, with his hand on my shoulder.

33
EPIPHANY

Late into the same Sunday morning I'm the only one awake. Dad flaked out in the sitting room wearing his guitar armour; Old Dear sprawled across their bed upstairs, fully clothed. She's snoring thickly, but I leave her door open in case she calls me. She's still up and down being sick.

Me? I've never known my head so clear. Since the cops left, something's happened: a weight, a burden, a pressure – I don't know – lifted away, leaving me more energised than a long-life battery. I actually feel positive; cheerful even. Which I can hardly believe, after all the garbage going down my chute the last few weeks.

I have – and I know what I'm saying because we discussed it one Circle Time – experienced epiphany.

From the moment I unlocked Grampa Dan's bedside cabinet and found what he had left me, I was changed forever.

Don't get your hopes up. There wasn't much to see. An old Bible. No cash. No treasure.

But the Bible; there lay my epiphany. I saw the light.

Got you worried, eh? Danny gone all happy-clappy born-again?

Fear not.

This is my Grampa Dan's Bible, remember. Well tatty, stained. Front cover hanging off. Manked up. You wouldn't want to touch it. It's small, hundreds of thin pages crackling a rip-warning when I turn them roughly. But I can't help my eagerness: there's something important for me on practically every page.

And I'm not talking about the Word of the Big Chief . . .

Faces. Faces. Faces. Each one totally distinct from the next, yet homogeneous as a shooting gallery of junkies because my Grampa Dan used his Bible to make a secret record of his fellow prisoners. He's drawn mostly in pencil so you have to screw up your eyes and ignore the text to see through to the fine detail of his art. Sometimes he uses ink, which bleeds out across the wafery paper, smudging over the printed words beneath.

These drawings: they're something else. The most

terrible and the most brilliant things I've ever seen. Hundreds of them filling the pages.

And folded into a concertina and fed down the spine of the Bible I found this larger picture: prisoners cluster in a semi-circle round this man's bald head. That's all you see of him. No body. Just a head, back view, sketched in very lightly as if it's hardly there. It sticks out the earth like it's planted.

Much more clearly drawn, clearer than anyone else in the sketch, is a figure in the foreground. A Japanese fella in uniform. Fat, four times broader than any of the raggedy wraiths around him, his trousers strain against the bulk of his thighs. He stands, legs spread Jakey-wide. Arms raised above his head, both hands clutching a descending sword.

FAT GUARD FOLLOWING ORDERS OF THE KEMPETAI.

is written in Grampa Dan's fine capitals underneath.

You want to see the black hate glittering out from this bloke's eyes. Sheer cold hate oozing from his expression. As palpable to me as it must have been for my Grampa

Dan when he watched the sword fall for real.

And later, in secret, recorded what he witnessed.

For me to find.

I tell you, I see that picture, and something inside me comes alive as if a touchpaper has fed a flame.

You must be thinking, how the heck can a Bible full of tortured men make someone feel good?

Unless that person was a total sicko.

Well, I *was* a sicko. Jakey's sicko puppet. No backbone of my own.

You always get guys like me, don't you?

Hangers-on. Following the leader even though the leader despises you for following. And *you* know and *he* knows it's only a matter of time before you're dumped. But it's too much effort to break away and stand up for yourself. Easier to be carried along until you're dropped. You know you're going to be dropped. It's all you deserve. If you're lucky, the concussion might knock some sense into you.

If you're unlucky, you might not get dropped at all . . .

You might get hunting-knifed in the back.

Like Ming . . .

The night Jakey was out to drop me.

Maybe I've been coming to my senses anyway. I'll never know that. All I can say is that the moment I open Grampa Dan's Bible I'm saved.

Reborn.

Alleluia.

AMEN.

I wish.

Unfortunately, everything's still topsy-turvy in Danny-world.

I have my epiphany. Even try to wake up Dad because I'm so chuffed about it: 'Look, Dad.'

I've ripped the photocopy of Posh Guru from my wall, hurtling downstairs with it and Grampa Dan's tape, and his bible.

'See these drawings, Dad? Look! You can't tell which is mine and which is Grampa's. I draw exactly like him. Same style, only I can get better because I'm being taught properly. And he knew. He wants me to be an artist . . . wants me to go to art school. He never had the chance himself . . . and look, Dad, I'm as good as he is . . . That's what he's been trying to tell me. Look, Dad. Please, Dad . . .'

My Old Dear doesn't seem interested either when I tell her about my epiphany. She waves me away, groaning, turning her back on me.

Just when I feel like talking.

34
BITING THE BULLET

It gets worse. First no one wants to talk to me, then I'm put in solitary confinement. It's true. End-of-year excitement in the summer air and where am I? Alone. Cooped in a windowless paper store connected to my new Heedie's room. I go to St Anne's now – Sanny's – Richard and Ali's school. Well, kind of. I'm serving my probation because – apparently – I'm 'not ready for the mainstream' yet. I'm taught in isolation and it's tough.

'No one in Sanny's gets a new jotter without my permission, and that's just the teachers I'm talking about, Hennessy,' CC, Sanny's Heedie (as in CCTV), warned me at the 'welcome' interview I attended with my folks. 'When a pencil's sharpened or a toilet's flushed in my establishment, Hennessy, I know, so don't even *think* of jiggery-pokery. I've had the cut of your jib for a long time.'

He's not bluffing. Sanny's has cameras everywhere: in the corridors, at every entrance and exit, outside each toilet block. If CC could square it with civil liberties he'd probably have cameras squinting up jacksies in the cubicles themselves.

I'm surprised I was even surprised when CC played me and my folks one of his playground tapes trained on the school gates. Said it had already been used by the cops to prove my association with Ming Mulholland. It filmed Jakey handing my money over to Ming that day outside Sanny's gates, me knocking his junk into the air. Apart from my gesture there was nothing to distinguish me from Jakey or Ming. Just another ned mooching for trouble.

An observation shared by my reluctant headmaster: 'Let's be clear, Hennessy. The police tell me you're not a bad lad, but I don't buy that. Far as I'm concerned, you mix with trash, that makes you trash. You've a long way to go to prove me wrong.'

For the first few weeks at Sanny's the only people allowed near me are the heads of department who set me assessments. I don't mix with any pupils, although when CC sends me out to the yard for blasts of fresh air out-with school intervals faces goggle me from every classroom.

One day I spot Richard and I'm so chuffed I give him a big wave, but there's only a half-smile of recognition from him before he turns away and I'm left wondering if he's been told to ignore me by his folks. Like Ali has. Not once since I started at Sanny's have I spoken to either of them. Haven't seen Richard since the night he lent me his mini disc. And that's odd.

If we met, I'd reassure him that he shouldn't worry; he'll only be stuck in the same year as me if there's a marked improvement in my grades. See, results of my assessments, apart from art and English, were 'unequivocally parlous', claims CC. So parlous that he hires an educational psychologist to check I haven't a major wiring fault that's been overlooked.

They dump me with this headshrink weedo. All beige corduroy and comb-over hairstyle.

Brian Uldoo I call him after he introduced himself with a constipated smile: 'I'm a qualified doctor, Danny, but Brian'll do.'

Complete dangleberry. I'm sorry, but it's true.

Three weeks I have sessions with him – test after test – and me with mountains of proper work to catch up with if I don't want to repeat third year. And I don't want to repeat. I can't afford to land up in all the dumbo sets again. If I want to get through the next three years and out, to art school, with a decent portfolio, I need to do the best I can. Starting now. Which is why I've no time for headshrink crap. I mean: four pages of equations to hand in before the end of the day and Brian Uldoo's got me studying frigging 'Inkblots, Brian.'

'Yes, inkblots, Danny, but I want you to tell me what *images* come into your head when I show you these patterns.'

'Inkblots, Brian.'

'No insects, or shapes or faces there?'

Course I see faces in the inkblots. Every one. Cheekbones, eye sockets, bags of bones. One blot was the spit of Grampa the day I found him dying. Another has staring eyes like Jakey.

But d'you think I'm going to screw the nut with a tosser like Brian Uldoo? No chance.

'Nuthin'. Blobs, Brian.'

'You're quite sure about that, Danny?'

I've yet to decide whether Brian abandons his tests and gets my file open in front of me – *Patient Background Report, Strictly Confidential* – because he figures that after three weeks of getting nowhere, I *am* thick.

Whatever his reason, Brian Uldoo gets his reaction from me at last when I read what's written about me in the file.

And I'm not just talking about Brian's casual jottings:

It's the lines and arrows worming over these comments until they converge at the tip of a gravestone shape Brian has doodled that puts my gas at a peep.

ROOTS???
DANIEL HENNESSY SNR,
DECEASED APRIL THIS YEAR
AGED 80
FORMER JAP POW!!!
WW2 TRAUMA/TORTURE UNRESOLVED
NO POST-WAR COUNSELLING ON RECORD

This is where I *start* to get angry, all right. I don't like the way Grampa's gravestone doodle jumps out at me from the page. What's he got to do with me repeating third year? I think, reading on. Then I'm really beeling.

Brian's jottings, see. They're not only about me.

PIVORCI

PAUL HENNESSY - Father/son
relationship poor - low self-esteem
Susan HENNESSY - attributes marital
breakdown to father-in-law

And there's all these notes covering the white paper around my folks' names:

- MARRIAGE GUIDANCE - unsuccessful
- DYSFUNCTIONAL FAMILY UNIT - Both Parties admit failure
- LACK STRATEGIES FOR DEALING WITH DANIEL JNR.
- SUSAN - Recent history of depression medication

'You've made this up,' I yell.

CC, who's heard me shouting from the other end of the corridor, has to hold me back. Pin my arms to my sides.

It's the biggest lie that upsets me the most. Doodled. Like it doesn't matter. All the way down the margin bracketing my folks' names:

↓
D
I   PAUL HENN
V   relationship p
O
R   Susan HENNE
C   breakdown to
I
N
G
≥

I mean, a qualified shrink, you think he'd have his basic bloody facts right?

'No way!' I scream into CC's face.

I tell him. Tell them both. It's not true. My folks haven't had a fight for weeks. Hell, we even had tea together the other night. There are never any arguments these days. And my Old Dear isn't moaning her face off that she's knackered running after Grampa Dan. I don't know how Brian can say she's depressed. Always out on the ran-dan with her mates. Dolled up. And Dad must be happy too. When he's in, he's playing his guitar. Loud. The nights Mum isn't clubbing, Dad plays a pub gig with his band. Must be having a ball, because he never comes home till way late. That's why my folks don't sleep in the same room any more. They don't want to disturb each other.

But they're not divorcing.

While I'm sitting in the quiet of CC's office counting to ten until my folks show to collect me, something Grampa Dan said comes back to me.

'Headshrinks? Interfering bampots the lot of them. You tell them nothin'.'

My head fills with his voice. I know now how he

must have been feeling. I wish I'd heard him out.

These shrinks the army organised had turned up. Out of the blue, Grampa thought, still not sussing that my folks had been opening his mail for the last ten years. My Old Dear had written back to them, deciding it would be *excellent* for psychiatrists to talk to Grampa about his war experiences. Probably do him the world of good.

So what? I thought at the time. You're lucky to get any visitors who can be arsed, listening to what you did sixty years ago, you old goat.

Apeshit, Grampa went. Bawling the house down long, long after he'd booted the shrinks out. Day and night, night and day this went on, non-stop bangbangbangbang.

'Who let these bastards in here? Asking if there's anything I need to get off my chest. What am I supposed to tell them: you jokers are sixty years too late. How did they get up here? Su-san? Paul? Danny? Someone talk to me . . .'

BANGBANGBANG.

It was constant. Caused my folks' most epic fight.

My Old Dear saying either Grampa Dan got sectioned or she walked.

My Old Boy actually put his foot down at that. No way, he insisted, was he sticking his dad in an asylum. Instead he struck a rare compromise with my Old Dear.

Had Grampa Dan put under sedation instead.

And he never came off it.

GRAMPA DAN'S LEGACY

35
FALSE MEMORY SYNDROME

Although Grampa Dan's been dead over a year, I spend ages talking to him these days. Sometimes aloud, especially when I'm up in the bedroom at my dad's. That's where I feel closest of all to Grampa. Well, it *is* his old room, not that you'd ever, ever know he'd lived here.

I say to Grampa, isn't it bollocks what Dad's done? Deleting every trace of you? No wardrobe, no chest of drawers, no record-player. All your clothes punted to Oxfam so none of your bedsmell lingers.

Grampa's been exorcised from Dad's life – a bit like someone else I could mention. That I'd better mention: she's still *my* Old Dear, after all, though she's history as far as Dad's concerned.

I have to hand it to good ol' Brian Uldoo: those notes of his were spot on. My folks *were* getting divorced. I only found out the way I did because – surprise, surprise! – between them they couldn't agree how to tell me without having a major barney about it. So they kept shtoom. I reckon I won my place in fourth year because CC felt so sorry for me: 'No wonder poor Daniel's upset, Mr Hennessy. Mrs Hennessy. This is a dreadful shock to the boy.'

Months on, my life has a new pattern. I shuttle between my folks and their irreconcilable differences, a do-it-yourself pass-the-parcel. Week nights at the Old Dear's, weekends back at . . .

Well, how can I describe my dad's place?

Not home.

I tell Grampa Dan: there's no place like home these days. It's definitely *not* the flat my Old Dear bought within spitting distance of Sanny's so I'll never have an excuse to be late for school again. Even though I get to nip back for lunch, even though I've got my own key, it's not home. From the first night I spent on my trendy new futon I felt uncomfortable, and it was nothing to do with the upholstery. I can't put my finger on it, but let's just say the Old Dear and myself have irreconcilable differences of our own which take up all the space between us, leaving no room to squeeze in conversation.

Silence like that is knackering.

I yearned for the clarty familiarity of my bedroom across the landing from the bigger room my folks shared, and next door to Grampa Dan . . .

Get home, Danny. Get the headphones on. Curl up like a shell under your duvet . . .

Well. Here's what I mean about not knowing where home is these days.

You know what happened in those first days I spent at the Old Dear's?

Not only did my dad sprout a ridiculous goatee, and finally come out as a baldie, but in my absence he let one of those home makeover teams run amok.

What else explains the dazzling white paint obliterating the match pot messages and psychedelic swirls of wallpaper that my dad could never be arsed to reach before?

'Like it, Danny?' he commanded, frog-marching me upstairs to admire – but not enter – the feng shui-ed minimalism of what was once my clarty sanctuary but which Dad has claimed as his room now.

'You're in Grampa's old room, Danny. Bigger. Got you a telly. Your mum'll love that. Ha!' were and remain his only comments on why a new broom – well, a new

Dyson – was panting for breath under the hall stairs.

Everything, mind you, I tell Grampa Dan, has changed this weather. Not just furniture and colour schemes. Life's so different from the way it was that sometimes I think I really *should* be seeing a headshrink. I've caught that False Memory Syndrome, convinced all these things happened in my past, only none of them did.

My folks were never together.

Grampa Dan never lived here.

I wasn't ever a pupil at the Academy.

And as for me and Ali Patel, we weren't ever . . .

The state of play between me and Ali Patel would confirm my False Memory Syndrome theory. She told me herself: 'There was never anything between us, Danny.'

I said, didn't I, that our friendship goes way back? From the day I met her, when we pulled our T-shirts up to count who had the most chicken-pox spots, and she let me join the dots into a lion on her tummy, all the way to the last time I was with her. A night, not three months ago. I haven't told anyone about this. Let's just say we'd our T-shirts pulled up again. It was hot. We were in the dark of her bedroom . . .

I swear, that night, her voice was husky in my ear. 'Danny, I'm finished with Richard. It's going to be great being together at Sanny's. I'll come back at lunchtimes to your mum's flat, Danny . . .'

False memories.

Ali Patel won't be giving me a dirty look, let alone a kiss. In school she glides past me with her mates and nothing, not one blink, not one glance, betrays a nanosecond history between us.

I blame the one part of my memory that I wish was false, only it's real. It came back to haunt me: probably the only time in his life Jakey's been good as his word. He got me as he said he would. Not with Nut's knife or the boot. What he did was worse.

I knew he was back in circulation, released from Young Offenders, because Sean broke third year ranks at assembly to give me my orders.

'Jakey's lookin' for you. Meet him up the park lunchtime.'

Although I rubbered Sean for weeks, I knew it was only a matter of time before Jakey lost patience. He was at a loose end, what with Waz off the scene at some boarding school, and Nut still in the pokey for stabbing

Ming. Jakey was sixteen. He'd quit school. Was signing on. Broke. Bored. Looking for playmates.

'You're dead if you don't make the park the day,' was Sean's final missive before Jakey broke cover.

I've wondered since if I should have met up with Jakey once, risking expulsion for truanting just to get him off my back.

But I couldn't do it. Not only because I was scared by the thought of Jakey's boot in my face. I daren't show him I could still be at his beck and call. Couldn't afford to let him see that. Not when I was getting out of the bit for the first time since I met him.

Grades creeping up.

Classmates chatting to me at intervals, asking me why I always went home for lunch. Inviting me to the canteen instead.

Not one punishment exercise to my name.

I wonder: would it have been worth sacrificing all that for one meeting with Jakey? Even if it meant he'd have left Ali alone?

I didn't dog off with Sean. Jakey was furious. It was raining. He couldn't hang out in the park, and he was locked out his own place. So he went to my Old Boy's, late afternoon, and waited for me there.

When I never showed – I'd history club – Jakey went ballistic. So Sean tells me the next day in school, pointing accusingly to his bruised cheek.

He really went mental, Sean said.

I know, I told him.

Ali Patel let me know already.

Not face to face. No chance of that ever, thanks to Jakey.

Ali hotmailed me to my dad's new laptop.

And my heart went into meltdown when I read You Have Mail from Ali-Oop. I was so chuffed: my first hotmail message that's not a pile of spam from some spam-head I've never met. Wonder why she didn't just phone me, I was thinking. Until I read my message.

Jakey bashed at Ali's door so hard that Mrs Patel thought someone was breaking in. 'Hey, you darkies,' he was shouting, 'any you golliwogs seen my mate Danny?'

When no one answered Jakey pissed through the letterbox.

When Ali chased him he spat on her.

Called her things I'm not going to say, even shouting

them through the window of the cop car Mrs Patel sent for. He was still insulting her while he was being cautioned and arrested for breach of the peace and possession of Class A gear.

That's why.

Me and Ali.

No chance.

Cheers, Jakey.

Thanks for the false memory.

36
THE BEGINNING OF THE BEGINNING

'You been in my salon before?'

Mister Derek, possibly even a little more roly-poly than the last time I saw him, months ago, cocks his head to one side like a robin with a mullet and purses his lips in concentration.

He's leaning over my shoulder to get a better squint at me through his mirror, frowning slightly when he can't place me in his client back-catalogue. He whisks out a red nylon cape, shaking it like a matador goading a bull: *Come on, you. Answer.*

He pauses just long enough to fix his blue stare on the eye-stripe peeping through my fringe. *Aye you've been here before*, says the smile twitching the corner of his mouth. His hands are heavy and knowing as he smooths the cape over my shoulders.

'Right, what can I do you for? Just get my lawnmower out, will I?'

In my head, memory stirs words, swirling them to the tip of my tongue.

I'm Danny, remember? I did what you said. Talked to Richard. My Grampa left a tape for me, and a Bible. Maybe he still wants to talk to me . . .

But if you think I open my mouth to let anything more than a few grunts escape, do I wheech. I shift in my chair, mumbling something about starting work in fifteen minutes so Derek's scissors'll take the hint.

'*That's* where I've seen you, Danny,' Mister Derek smiles, although I still haven't ever told him my name. 'Now that boss of yours in Vibes, *he* needs a trim.'

Loads of times today, when there's been nothing doing in Vibes, I've thought of nipping back to see Mister Derek. I want to ask him: does Grampa Dan know what's happened to me? Is he pleased? Is he proud?

See, I'm getting a prize. Hence the shearing. Monday afternoon I'll be on stage in front of the whole school, and it won't be in a Usual Suspects parade of smokers, or bullies, or neds.

I'll be getting a clap, a handshake from CC, a merit

certificate. Both my folks are invited to see me. CC'll need to turn his central heating up; this'll be the first time they've been in spitting distance of each other since the last afternoon in CC's office when I freaked out with Brian Uldoo.

Believe it or not, this merit is my second prize this month. Couple of weeks ago, a letter arrives. Dad's handwriting. I open the thing and a cheque for seventy-five quid flutters out – *Pay Daniel Hennessy* – with a note from my Old Boy:

Congratulations, Danny. We'll celebrate when I see you at the weekend. Curry?
Dad

I'm delighted, of course, but when I see Dad's note, for one minute this thought rips through me like a slash from Nut's knife: Dad won't phone me at my Old Dear's flat in case she picks up. I mean, even Miss West phones me. Now there's a sweet surprise. Because Danny the Dumpling has only won second prize in a national art competition! Out of thousands and thousands and thousands of entries; every secondary school in the UK. Couldn't believe it. I'd completely forgotten about Miss West entering my Posh Guru drawing into a competition. A lifetime ago now.

'Keep it up, Danny,' Miss West says. 'I'd love to get a look at your art school portfolio. We should meet for a chat. Hearing stunning reports from Matt Sillars.'

Miss West's been hearing right. That's why I'd love to know that Grampa Dan knows . . .

My Old Dear's way more impressed by the merit award than the art money.

'You did that drawing in the past,' she says, 'but the merit's about your future, Danny.'

She's completely wrong, my Old Dear. If I wanted to be thrawn, I could argue that the only reason I'm winning anything is because I'm not letting go of the past. Grampa Dan's past. But with that Prozac bringing out my Old Dear's rottweiler tendencies, I'm not going to argue with her.

But I'll explain what I mean about not letting go of the past.

See, Richard wanted Grampa Dan's tape back, and instead of me handing it over like it was no big deal, I challenged him.

'What d'you want it for?' I asked.

When he told me, I said, no way.

Well, he'd some notion to donner round the dinner hall with his latest girlfriend, Gillian the Brain, in tow, lugging the video cam. They'd play wee bits of Grampa Dan's testimony, like they were running a guess the mystery voice competition, and ask pupils for their reactions.

'It's the Inter-schools History Club project,' Richard explained. 'Secrets and Scars: Our Ignorance, Their Reality.'

When I heard that, I told Richard, no way are you serving up my Grampa's nightmare in throwaway dollops between chip butties. Who's going to take the tape seriously? Everyone'll be mucking about, not listening. Taking the mick out of Grampa's voice. You'll need to come up with something better than that, I said, before I let you use my tape. Must be the first time I've cared enough about anything to put my foot down.

Anyone else but Richard would have pulled out his *wait a minute here, pal, who recorded Grampa Dan in the first place?* trump. But he didn't.

'Danny, I'm sorry,' he apologised. 'You're right. Dumb idea. It's just that we're pushed for time. I can't think of a better way to make an impact . . . get people thinking . . .'

Well, who knows why things happen sometimes. What's for you won't go by you, Grampa Dan used to say, although I never understood what the heck he meant till now.

'I've an idea . . .' I volunteered. No big deal. Made a few pretty bleeding-obvious suggestions, that's all.

We got this multi-media installation set up in an empty classroom. Richard said it was much better than wandering around with a tape. Pupils came to us, but only if they were interested. No time wasters. No chancers. No Jakeys.

Hardly rocket science, but this is what earned me my imminent merit certificate. My 'commendable input', CC called it.

As far as I'm concerned, only Grampa's input was commendable.

And the artwork. It was mega: I sorted that.

And oi, before you think that seventy-five-quid prize has me thinking I'm Rembrandt, hear me out. My artwork was mega because I didn't do it. *He* did it: my Grampa Dan. I had his Bible and I copied out some of his pictures. I did it in one sitting, listening over and over to his tape and – I know this sounds screwy – but I concentrated so hard on getting everything right that I felt Grampa Dan was guiding my hand.

So he did it. Not me. The only prize he ever won. About bloody time too!

There was one drawing I could never have copied though: the execution of Sammy Orr by Fat Guard. Instead, I asked Computing if we could scan Grampa Dan's original and blow it up as close to lifesize as we could get it. I tell you, when you saw it like that . . . gobsmacking. It became the centrepiece of the project. You walked in and there was this giant image all fuzzy with loss of resolution so you *thought* you knew what you were looking at, but you had to put on headphones and hear Grampa Dan explain what was going on before you knew you really were seeing what you thought you were seeing. Clever, eh? Stopped you in your bloody tracks.

There was music too, playing in the background. Guess what it was?

Clue: I made a permanent donation to the project.

Well, I don't play Skarrs this weather. Reminds me of – ach, you know what . . .

You know who . . .

It was Richard's idea to use it, and we'd to clear it with CC first. I tell you, I was squirming while Seth Lamprey effed and blinded his way through 'Torture Chamber' and 'Kommandant', and CC cocked his ear, frowning at the lyrics on the CD: 'Lads, I really don't think we can let our junior pupils hear . . .'

Give Richard his due, he insisted on using Skarrs. Sometimes it's appropriate to shock, and what could be better, he argued, all flushed and earnest, to contrast ignorant poison like *this*, with the reality of real suffering? Anyone with half a brain would get the message.

'It's a great way to make people who don't think think.'

People like me, eh?

Funny how I've gone off the whole Skarrs scene. Richard was right: two chords and a load of swearing.

These days, anyway, I'm into all sorts of music. Blues.

R'n'B. Leadbelly. Howlin' Wolf. Rory Gallacher. Hendrix.

It's not like I've much choice. Unless I wear heavy-duty earplugs I'm forced to absorb everything Vibes' sound system pumps out while I'm working there on Saturdays for Huck. Not that I'm complaining. Quite the opposite, in fact. I can't get over how much of the leather-jacket clone music I dig. Listen to me: *dig*. Must be getting old. Or wise. That what Dad says. I hear a new voice and it's like another epiphany. I'm like *wow, who's that?* Seriously. I have to stop whatever I'm doing, stacking a shelf or tracing something obscure on the computer – and I freeze. Like Grampa Dan, when Ella or Peggy or Hoagy or Louis or Bing sang to his soul.

Nina Simone.

Otis Redding.

Janis Joplin.

Van Morrison.

Jim Morrison.

Billie Holiday.

Aretha Franklin.

Jackie Wilson.

Sam Cooke . . .

I keep thinking I've made a new discovery, and I grab

my dad when he comes to meet me every Saturday. 'Have you heard this album, Dad?' I ask. And he laughs.

Him and Huck. Pair of them laugh like drains.

I mean, Dad already owns every album I ask him about. It's in his collection. Always was. Music at my fingertips. Could have been, *should* have been getting into it years ago.

When it was easier.

Instead of . . .

Well. In the words of Bob Dylan, another of my recent discoveries, *Things Have Changed*.

Or am I just being too naff for my own good now, name-checking a song with even more history? *The times they are a'changin'*.